Love Has The Best Intentions

Christine Arness

S

Published by
Satin Romance
An Imprint of Melange Books, LLC
White Bear Lake, MN 55110
www.satinromance.com

Love Has the Best Intentions ~ Copyright © 2015 by Christine Arness

ISBN: 978-1-68046-042-1

Names, characters, and incidents depicted in this book are products of the author's imagination or are used fictitiously. Any resemblance to actual events, locales, organizations, or persons, living or dead, is entirely coincidental and beyond the intent of the author or the publisher. No part of this book may be reproduced or transmitted in any form or by any means, electronic or mechanical, including photocopying, recording, or by any information storage and retrieval system, without permission in writing from the publisher.
Published in the United States of America.

Cover Art by Angela Archer

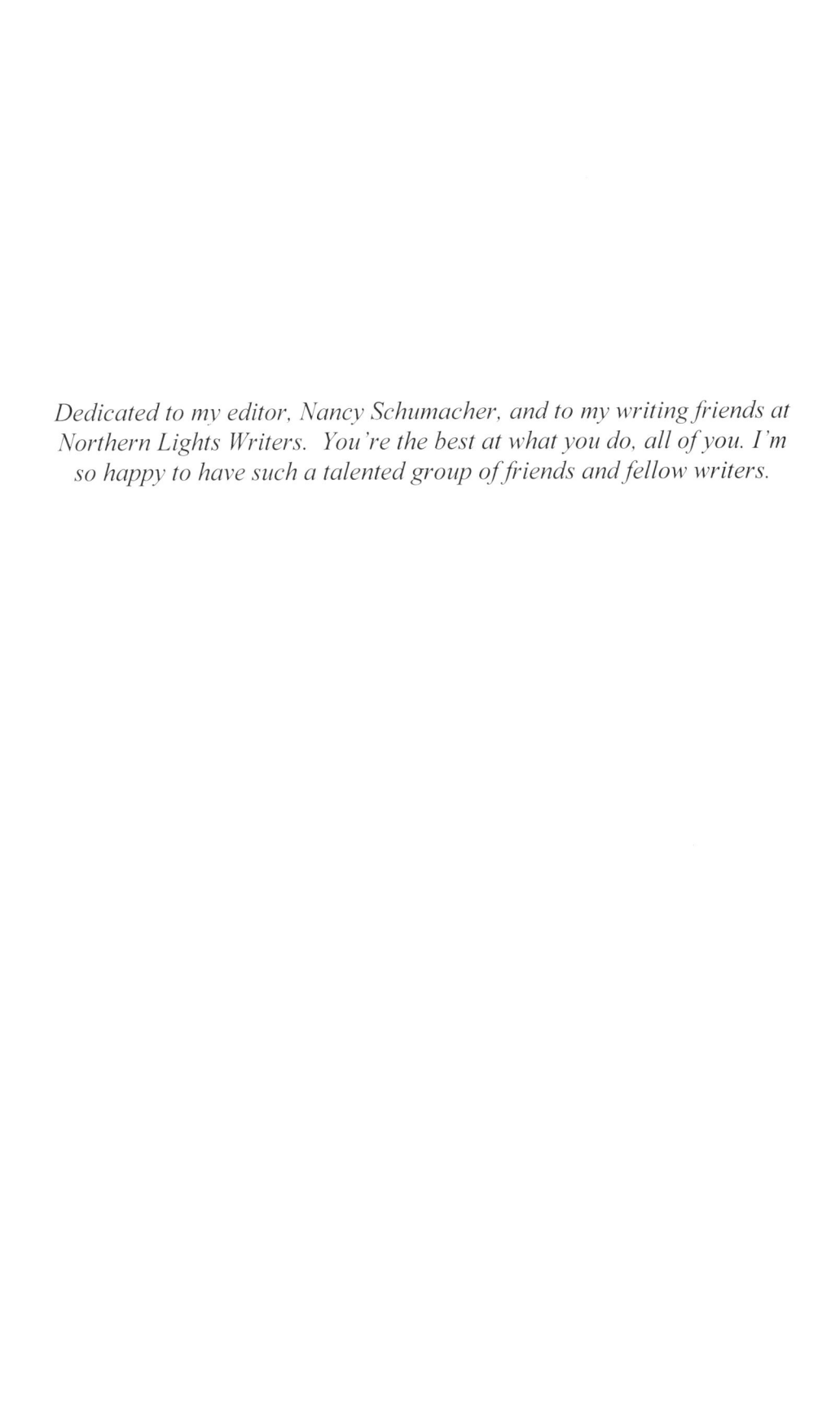

Dedicated to my editor, Nancy Schumacher, and to my writing friends at Northern Lights Writers. You're the best at what you do, all of you. I'm so happy to have such a talented group of friends and fellow writers.

Love Has the Best Intentions

Puppies from Heaven
An artist working in his home studio finds a new direction for both his art and his love life when a young woman who operates a puppy training center moves next door.

Love to Go
An order gone wrong at a big city pizzeria starts out as humiliating but ends up as love filled experience for a small town girl.

Perfect Body – Perfect Match
Trying too hard to achieve a perfect body, Becca nearly forgot the importance of being herself.

Flutter of Wings
Gail's matchmaking skills go awry when she arranges for a date with an acquaintance and, too late, realizes he's her perfect match.

When Hearts Collide
Kate's intentions to meet her knight in shining armor undergo a change when their cars collide.

At Home to Roost
Rosemary's intentions to make the holiday perfect for her family go astray when an ice storm causes a power failure.

Harvest Gold
A young mother realizes her grief over losing the contents of their home in a fire is keeping her from starting new memories with her family.

Case in Point
A young divorce attorney realizes the heartache she's experiencing in her practice is causing her disillusionment about marriage.

Honey, Do You Love Me?

Claire must make a decision whether to keep her unborn child or lose the man she loves.

The Friendship Ring
Linda threw away her high school sweetheart's declaration of love. Years later, she returns home and finds both a refuge and another chance at love.

Sleeping with Dr. Dee
A couple's marriage struggles due to not enough hours in the day and they seem to be growing in different directions. Then an innocent remark by one of their children starts a nasty rumor circulating but, strangely enough, it also starts the healing process.

Half of My Heart
Jenny receives a letter from her husband written just before he died in combat. This letter takes her on a journey to an orphanage in France where she finds half of her heart.

Short and Sweet
Charlotte's embarrassment over her father's fun loving personality changes to pride when she glimpses the joy he brings into the lives of others.

Puppies from Heaven

My life changed, irrevocably, when she rang the doorbell. I was out and Burt, my tenant, has been known to snore through tornados, garbage truck collisions, and Mrs. Barnstable's practice sessions for her opera lessons. But as an EMT working the midnight shift, he's conditioned to always respond to bells.

Fate could have been thwarted by some incisive questioning when Burt brought up his angelic visitation, but I decided to be humorous instead. "Describe this celestial being."

"She had glossy black hair and the most heavenly blue eyes," he murmured dreamily.

"And what did our special visitor want?" Convinced Burt was pulling my leg, I played along.

"She had a clipboard. I remember signing a paper."

"No doubt you ordered angel hair pasta, Girl Scout cookies or something equally divine. Face it, pal, you dreamed up your dream girl."

Burt frowned. "But I can still see that angelic smile …"

The nape of my neck prickled, but as a graphic artist/painter, I have enough daydreams without analyzing Burt's. Original Harrisons were beginning to shuffle out of the gallery which displays my work and a fall showing had been scheduled. My ambition is to become self-supporting with my brush, even if it means living in a tent.

No danger of that at the moment, however. I own a brownstone in a Chicago suburb, a gift from my parents upon their migration to Florida.

Burt rents the upstairs; we share kitchen privileges. For me, the main attraction spans the back of the house, a sunroom with marvelous eastern lighting, which faces a yard enclosed by a box hedge that's murder to keep properly trimmed.

Mrs. Barnstable occupies the house to the right. After Mr. B's demise, his widow broadened her horizons in all directions, with opera lessons, learning to quilt, and ballroom dancing, among other pursuits.

My neighbors on the left had sold their house and moved out weeks ago. I was yet to meet the new owner as I spent every spare moment, when I wasn't working as a freelance graphic artist, preparing for my fall show titled "City Glimpses". My newest effort featured a wizened vendor at Wrigley Field. Using a zoom lens effect, I had focused attention on gnarled hands clutching peanut bags with the background blurred into a collage of Cub caps.

Nearly a month after Burt's "visitation", I was back in my studio. The sunroom's placement and the hedges filtered out most street noises, so I was startled to hear a bark. A glance at the yard revealed only a carpet of rippling green velvet, but the yap was repeated.

Convinced I had a trespasser, I jammed my brush into a jar and stalked outside. Standing in ankle-high grass, I surveyed the yard and felt foolish. The phantom dog remained invisible; the breeze tickled my face, scented with Mrs. Barnstable's roses. Another yip! Pasting a fresh frown on my face, I strode over to demand that my new neighbors keep their puppy quiet.

I thrust my scowling features over the hedge, pricking the underside of my jaw as my mouth dropped open. A girl sat upon the grass surrounded by what appeared to be rejects from the cast of *101 Dalmations.* A noisy dispute suddenly erupted between a white mop and a black mop over a plastic carrot.

"Play with your own toy." The girl extended a ring to the black mop.

"Is your Mom or Dad home?"

The girl rose. Hair as glossy and black as a raven's wing (excuse the artistic license) swirled around a tanned cheek.

"You must be Harrison. I've met Burt." Her smile forgave me for mistaking her for a child. "I'm Fiona Flynn."

Pride being a besetting sin of mine, I resented that grin. "Well, Ms.

Flynn, keep your yapping brats quiet. I'm trying to concentrate."

Her smile faded. "These brats are my clients and this is exercise period."

My turn to yelp.

She looked puzzled. "If you had any objections to a puppy day care center, you should have spoken up earlier."

"Earlier? This is the first I've heard of this insanity!"

"Working people don't have time to raise or train a puppy. I provide a vital service for them."

I felt my whole body swell with anger. "It may be necessary, but I don't want it next door."

Suddenly noticing her absence, the crew stopped squabbling. They milled and whined until White Mop spotted Fiona and led the pack over to her. The yipping chorus broke out again; the pups were as glad to see her as kids who'd lost sight of their mom in a crowded store.

Fiona's lips moved, but I couldn't hear her over the din. She put her mouth near my ear and a tingle zinged down my spine. "I did bring this issue up already with the neighbors. Burt signed the petition for my home business permit!"

"But he had no right—" Heavenly blue eyes. Burt's angel! "Was his hair sticking up and was he extremely agreeable?"

"He was very polite." Unlike you, her frown implied.

"A document signed by a sleepwalker won't stand up in court. Besides, he's only a tenant."

"Burt was asleep?" Fiona laughed, a chime of celestial bells. "Nice try, but you'll have to think of something else. I've spent too much money buying and converting this place."

"I refuse to live next door to a nursery!" My shout silenced the clamoring horde.

"Good luck finding a new place," Fiona said, giving me a sweetly triumphant smile. "Come, children, nap time!"

Round one to Fiona. The pack didn't watch my dignified retreat, instead they chose to waddle after their favorite person.

I didn't have the cash or the stomach for hiring an attorney, so after a cooling off period, I resolved to try to get along and make the best of the situation. But Fiona and her flea circus did their best to make their presence felt. I struggled to complete "The Vendor" but it was always feeding time, play-time, or just plain noise time next door.

Each morning, relays of cars brought the pooches while I hovered by my front window, drinking coffee and glaring. The regulars soon became familiar and, if pressed, I'd have to admit a liking for a perky terrier with a wiry salt and pepper coat.

Once having made a stand, however, I determined not to back down, no matter how lonely my perch. My sense of isolation was heightened when Mrs. Barnstable had Burt and I over for supper and I had to listen to a bass and contralto duet singing Fiona's praises.

While passing out napkins folded into swans, my hostess divulged that Fiona had left veterinary college to care for her dying mother, had never married, and adored children.

"All right, she's a saint. An angel!" I sent a sour look in Burt's direction. "But I doubt whether she can make a living babysitting mutts."

"She charges $80-$120 per week per pup, Harrison, depending upon the training package."

I drew a mental sketch of the group and counted wet noses. "She's got at least twelve dogs—probably a grand a week! It took me over a year to sell $1,000 worth of paintings!"

"A lovely girl. So sweet, so kind," Mrs. Barnstable gushed and I wondered whether she'd taken up matchmaking as a new hobby.

If so, Burt would have hired her in a minute. He spent more and more of his time off over at Fiona's while I grappled with my illusive muse and fumed.

The crisis occurred a miserably hot afternoon several weeks later as I stared at The Vendor, gripped by the conviction that my creative juices had dried up completely.

As a background to this self-castigation, I heard Fiona's clear voice drilling the troops. "Sit, Bugs. No, honey, I said sit—not wet. Try again. Halifax, put down that stick. Tree bark makes you sick. Bugs, sit!"

In frustration, I hurled my brush against the wall, leaving a jagged blue check mark. Jumping off my stool, I shoved open the sliding screen door. I had a bone to pick with the ruler of those bone gnawing mops.

Fiona sat tailor fashion on the grass. The sun's bright fingers picked out the blue-black highlights in her hair, reminding me of a grackle's plumage.

Canine pupils surrounded her, some dozing on the grass, others quarrelling over toys, while Bugs, a pop-eyed bull dog, did his best to please. As Fiona gave the command, he lowered his head until his jaw rested on the grass and squinted up at her hopefully.

"Wrong end, baby." Fiona scooped him up and tickled him behind the ears. "But I'm proud of you."

He drooled happily as she cuddled him. My own eyes popped as I realized how much I envied Bugs!

The terrier sounded an intruder alert and Fiona raised her head. "Quiet, guys and gals! The Grinch is back."

She strolled over while I attempted to maintain the appropriate expression of an Outraged Artist. "What's the complaint this time?"

"I can't work!"

"Surely, you don't blame me for high unemployment rates." Her smile was wickedly demure. "We're staying on our side."

"But the noise isn't."

Her smile became penitent. "I'm sorry. I try to keep it down to a dull roar. They're quiet at nap time."

"I can't make a living painting an hour or two a day!"

Fiona looked troubled. "I'm afraid that I'm used to the country and no near neighbors. Why don't we discuss this over some freshly squeezed lemonade?"

Part of me—let's face it, 98%--wanted to hurdle the hedge and rush into the house with Fiona, slamming the door in the pups' faces. But pride held me back with a firm grip on my shoulders while jealousy clutched at my ankles. She'd already conquered Burt with that smile; a Harrison was made of sterner stuff. Besides, if I weakened, the prospect of my fall show might dissolve, along with my dream.

"If any of your critters sets a paw in my yard, I'll swear out a nuisance complaint and close you down, Ms. Flynn."

It didn't take Fiona's stricken expression to tell me I'd gone too far, and all I had left was my pride.

I slunk back to my easel, but The Vendor no longer excited me. Other images invaded my brain, filling my head with swirls of color, and I recognized the symptoms of an "art attack", a period when I'm racked by a fever that won't let me rest until I capture, on canvas, the pictures crowding into my mind.

Propping The Vendor in the corner, I stretched a fresh canvas and arranged it on the easel. When Burt came home the next morning, he found me, unshaven and bleary-eyed, frantically trying to capture the vision which oppressed me.

He hovered in the doorway, his voice concerned. "Another art attack? You're going to kill yourself. One day I'll find you lying dead in a pool of Vermillion #2."

I said nothing, willing him to leave.

"Just one question, old buddy, closed or open casket?"

"Out!" I slung a paint-smeared rag in his direction.

Hours later, I unclenched my death grip on the brush. In the midst of City Glimpses would be my masterpiece: "Summer Interlude." Drinking in the heady colors and delicate brush strokes, I became aware of a persistent scratching noise and turned.

The Cairn Terrier pup peered in through the screen door. "Lost, little fella?"

Various muscle groups saw fit to remind me that they'd been locked into the same position for nearly twenty-four hours. Stifling a groan, I slid open the door. The pup trotted in and flopped down, resting his head on my sneaker with a gusty sigh.

"Harrison, Fiona's lost a pup." Burt halted in the studio doorway.

Fiona ducked around him and burst into my sanctuary. "You found Kirby! I was so worried."

Kirby's stubby tail wagged a greeting, but he didn't move.

"Bad Kirby! I've told you not to go near the hedge. I'm sorry, Harrison. He must have tunneled under—" Fiona broke off. "Are you all right?"

I suddenly realized I'd been able to concentrate despite the noise. Fiona, not the pups, had been responsible for my painter's block. My knees turned to jelly.

The angel visitant caught sight of the painting and froze. "Harrison!"

She stared, open mouthed, forcing me to stagger unaided over to a chair. Humming, "I've Got a Date with an Angel," Burt disappeared.

I studied my newest work of art, which depicted a woman seated on the grass. Her hair as dark as a raven's wing and eyes a heavenly blue, she smiled down on the pups surrounding her. A pop-eyed bulldog had its rear end coyly elevated while a rough-coated terrier leaned trustfully against its mistress.

"Harrison, I've been guilty of disturbing you. I'm so sorry. I guess I never realized what a talented artist lived next door."

I could only smile at the compliment. Unshaven, exhausted and blissfully happy.

Fiona crouched beside me. She smelled of sunshine, grass, and summer breezes. "I didn't think you liked me or the dogs! But this, this was painted with such love—"

As she spoke the last word, our eyes met and she blushed. "I think I should get Kirby back to his buddies."

"One of your dogs set a paw in my yard, Fiona."

She gazed at me blankly until remembrance of my threat to close down her school colored her face rosy pink. "Harrison, if you call the police, I'll, I'll …"

"You'll what? Set Kirby on me?"

The beast thus referred to licked my outstretched hand.

Fiona sighed. "I should have boarded attack dogs."

Lust has never been as pure as the desire I felt for my companion. "In return for my tolerance, you must pay a forfeit."

"A forfeit?"

I placed a kiss on the lips I had so meticulously reproduced on canvas. The ensuing embrace progressed nicely until needles sank into the flesh just above my shoe.

"I think Kirby's jealous," Fiona apologized as she pried the puppy off my ankle.

"Such an interesting hypothesis. Shall we conduct further tests?" Rejuvenated, I moved toward Fiona, but she retreated, that adorable blush coloring her face again.

"Oh, dear, I've got to get back before my mob of fuzzy hooligans breaks into the cookie jar and gets sick from eating too many puppy treats."

"We wouldn't want that, darling Fiona. But would you consider going out to supper with me tonight?"

Her answering smile was as divine as the blue of her eyes.

"I'll be over at seven o'clock." I limped after her to the front door. "Will all the mutts be picked up by then?"

"All except Kirby. He's mine." Fiona stood on tiptoe to bestow a butterfly-light kiss on my cheek. "But I'm willing to share him. See you at seven. We've got fences to mend in our relationship—starting with that escape tunnel Kirby made under your hedge."

Then she was gone, leaving me gaping after her on the doorstep as Burt must have done the morning of our first otherworldly visitation. My angel with her own guardian imp.

I hobbled back inside. If Kirby didn't mend his manners when I tried to steal another kiss, I knew of one picture in my fall show that would have a certain terrier painted out of it.

THE END

Love To Go

Jenny and I blew into Corleone's Pizzeria just ahead of the approaching storm. I immediately felt its coziness envelop me. "Brick ovens make all the difference in texture and taste," I informed Jenny, my words tumbling over each other as I inhaled the scents of yeast and toasted cheese.

A small town girl, I've only been in the big city for a few months. Jenny's a co-worker who heard me bragging about finding a fabulous restaurant and decided to tag along. Since stumbling across the pizzeria, I'd visited the place nearly every week. Watching the family members who owned Corleone's and listening to their banter and laughter made me feel somehow less lonely.

I steered Jenny to a small red table whose round top resembled a piece of pepperoni. "Here's the order slip. They'll pick it up after you check off what you want. FYI, when it's ready, they announce your choice to the room, usually with teasing comments."

"Then I'll order something non-fattening." Jenny smoothed her hair and glanced around the intimate interior. "I see there's mostly families in here tonight, RaeLynn. This doesn't look like such a great place to meet guys."

It's not a 'meet' market, it's more of a 'meat' market—remember, I only claimed that the pizza's great." I avoided looking for Nicky behind the counter. He worked Friday evenings and somehow on Fridays I usually found myself hungry for pizza. And a slice of Nicky.

The door blew open and the man himself burst in, threading his way between the tables.

In a moment, Jenny would spot him—she's got a laser scope that locks on any cute guy in the vicinity, which meant I was crazy for bringing her along.

I snatched up a slip and waved it under her nose. "Wouldn't it be wonderful if we could order dates to specifications?" In the "special order" section, I printed the first item on my list of wants and wishes. "Dazzling smile—one that makes me weak in the knees."

"You go with the guy with a good dental plan," Jenny muttered. "I'd rather have one whose killer body does the talking for him."

But Nicky was more than just eye candy. I'd watched him mop floors, hand toss pizza dough like a pro and listen to complaints without ever losing his sparkle. By nibbling on my pizza slices to prolong each visit and eavesdropping on the chatter behind the counter, I'd learned Nicky took college courses several evenings a week, chasing his dream of becoming an accountant.

I looked up in time to see him bend down to retrieve a doll and hand it back to a tot who gazed up at him, wide-eyed. He said something that made her giggle. I giggled too, reminded of my next requirement and started to write again. "Good with kids—I want a big family."

I thought we were talking about a date, not a commitment." Jenny scowled at the choices on the order blank. "No pineapple. They don't offer many low fat options."

"Not low fat, but life long," I whispered. "Like the type of marriage my parents experienced."

"Okay, I'm out of here." Jenny stood up and shook back her hair with an impatient gesture. "If I decide to eat three kinds of cheese and bacon on my pizza, I'm gonna do it some place where they don't announce my choices to the world—"

When she sank back down, her mouth slightly open, I realized she must have caught sight of Nicky at the microphone.

I scribbled down my final item. "Eyes a rich espresso brown."

The man's husky baritone cut through the chatter. "Who's got #31? Hint: it's a pie Popeye would love!"

At a corner table, a couple waved to the room at large. "Spinach pizza. I yam what I yam!" the guy hollered amidst a fresh burst of laughter.

Love To Go

I snatched up another slip and with quick slashes checked the boxes for my usual order. Nicky's sister appeared at our table just as the door opened again, the wind swirling our slips and a napkin to the floor. I dove for the orders and handed them over to Mara, crumpling my wish list in my other hand.

Nicky continued to entertain the patrons with his good natured comments while I pretended not to watch and clutched my "order". If only I had the guts to talk to him. If only Nicky would notice me watching him …

Then Mara, a smile teasing her lips, handed the next slip to her brother, who announced, "#38's ready—and, wow! Listen up, folks, someone's ordered a great smile, a person equally good with kids and numbers, and they're looking for a lifetime commitment and dark brown eyes. And they want it 'to go'. Sounds like we've got a marriage proposal here tonight, folks!"

Everyone applauded, along whistles and shouts. Mara smiled at me while I sat as stiff as a wooden artifact in a museum, thoughts flashing like traffic signals in my brain. She must have recognized my writing, remembered me handing the slip to her. No. Not possible. I must be asleep; this had turned into a nightmare.

Nicky flashed that grin at the now silent crowd, everyone craning their necks to see who was about to go down on bended knee.

Jenny, traitorous Jenny, gestured at me. "Over here, over here!"

I hated her.

Nick ignored her piping voice. "Now speak up, who's the romantic fellow—"

He broke off when his sister grabbed his sleeve, gestured in my direction and whispered in his ear. Nicky stared at the order again before his shocked gaze met mine. I gasped, unfolding the wadded paper in my fist. Oh, no! I was holding my actual pizza order, not my wish list.

Jenny burst out laughing. Covering my face with my fingers, I wanted to sink under the table and die, in no particular order.

After an eternity, someone gently moved my hands; I stared into espresso dark eyes. The restaurant noise faded as the world shrunk to just Nicky and me.

"Our advertising promises that we'll serve exactly what the

customer orders. Shall we discuss your special specifications?"

A shiver ran through my body as he brushed a strand of hair back from my face and plucked my regular order from my nerveless fingers, replacing it with my wishes and wants.

I gulped and stuttered, frozen in fear. Then Nicky smiled the smile I adored, the one that makes me weak in the knees.

I wanted to tell him how much I'd longed to talk to him, how his smiles had warmed my lonely heart. Then from somewhere I got the courage to pick up the shaker of parmesan flakes and sprinkle it on his dark curls.

"If you recall, my usual order calls for extra cheese." He chuckled and I couldn't stop an answering smile from stretching my lips. "Let's go for coffee at the diner across the street," I whispered. "Tonight, for a change, I asked for my order to go."

THE END

Perfect Body—Perfect Match

Becca was in pursuit of the American Dream. She craved what every man and woman secretly yearns for—a perfect body and someone to appreciate it.

Her best friend, Lana, had a perfect body. Becca sometimes wondered if Lana had ever endured the pimples and awkwardness of adolescence. She appeared to have stepped, fully grown, from the pages of a fitness magazine advertising French cut leotards. Whenever Lana walked down the street, men forgot urgent appointments, slammed into traffic light standards and drooled on their silk ties.

If Becca hadn't acquired a perfect body yet, it wasn't for lack of trying. One of her recent ventures into the realms of fitness was the purchase of an exercise bike. After a week of nightly workouts, however, she came to the conclusion that her own seat was completely incompatible with that of the bicycle's.

Next, Becca bought several fitness DVDs. The shapely women on the covers were frozen in mid-movement and the clincher for Becca was their happy smiles. She spent the next month sweating, bumping into furniture and "going for the 'burn'. The day she found herself sneaking out of the room when the instructor's back was turned to brew a cup of herbal tea was the day the fitness DVDs were banished to a cupboard.

As she perched in her cubbyhole at the studio, sketching designs for a toilet paper campaign and nibbling M&M's, Becca dreamed of possessing a body where dimples peeped coyly near her mouth instead of her knees. So she signed up for a YMCA rebounder class, hoping to obtain the benefits of jogging without the dangers posed by dogs, cars and pedestrians.

Memories of that rebounder class fiasco still gave Becca a guilty twinge. Bouncing in unison with ten other women, she began to feel almost weightless, no longer trapped within the folds of cellulite.

After a few minutes of gentle jogging, the instructor encouraged them to step up their heart rate. "Jump, girls, jump! Take it higher and higher. Pretend you're a ballerina floating gracefully into the air."

Even though she had a wonderful imagination, she couldn't see herself floating in a tutu. Becca had always felt more in tune with animals, so she pictured herself instead as a jack rabbit. Bounding along a dusty path and keeping a sharp rabbit eye out for coyotes, she sprang into the air but, unfortunately, her trajectory must have been slightly askew.

Like a rocket gone off course, Becca soared up and across the neighboring rebounder, taking its occupant with her on a path of errant flight.

Mrs. McCarthy suffered multiple bruises, especially on her ample rear portions, while Becca ended up with a badly sprained ankle. When the next brochure from the YMCA arrived in the mail, someone had used a red marker to slash through the rebounder class. She suspected the change had been made exclusively on her copy.

Over orange blossom tea on a Sunday afternoon, Lana suggested a solution to Becca's quest for that perfect body. "Join my health club, The Fitness Studio. You can lift weights, work out on state of the art machines, swim ... all with the aid of a personal instructor. The men are real foxes!" Lana leaned back on the kitchen chair, drew a deep breath and crossed elegantly sculpted legs. "I get all the personal attention I need."

"I'll bet you do," Becca muttered, tearing an envious gaze from her friend's shapely limbs. Her own legs would never reach that length, but if the rest of her body would cooperate, she might possibly aspire to become a pocket Venus.

"Come with me to The Fitness Studio tomorrow night," Lana urged. "You'll love the new you that you become."

Becca picked up a calico ball of fluff named Lady BoJangles, and scratched her cat companion behind the ears. She had to face facts:

Perfect Body—Perfect Match

exercising her creativity each day hadn't taken an inch off her hips. Her lack of commitment might stem from not investing enough money in a program. Perhaps if she splurged an entire year's food budget on leotards and walked to work because her car had been sold to pay The Fitness Studio dues ...

Lana, dramatically attired in a scarlet leotard, mini wrap skirt and matching leg warmers, led the way into The Fitness Studio. Two men in the process of picking up their cards to leave immediately surrendered them again and one dropped his shoes on the floor with a thud. A third man squeezed the can of racquet balls he was holding so tightly that the lid flew off.

During her interview, Becca was asked about her goals in joining the club. She swallowed the wish of gaining a traffic-stopping body and murmured a few words about needing to get back into shape, thus implying at one time she had been a pocket Venus.

The woman conducting the interview kindly concealed her disbelief under a warm smile and summoned a statuesque blond to take Becca on a tour of the facilities. As a confirmed pizza-for-breakfast person, Becca had trouble warming up to a guide with the radiant complexion of one who considers yogurt and alfalfa sprouts junk food.

The machine room was crammed with bikes, steppers, ski simulators, rowing machines, etc., all controlled by electronic brains and equipped with more choices than a Surface or Tablet.

Forcing a smile, she clung to high hopes for the next stop, only to find the blue tiled pool awash with muscular shoulders and arms cleaving the water as dedicated dolphins swam laps with the concentration of hamsters in an exercise wheel. The splashing reminded Becca of watching a shark attack in a horror movie.

After touring the weight rooms, relaxation center (sauna and massage) and aerobics areas, the women returned to the office. Becca's guide, barely concealing her desire to wash her hands of this couch potato who had apparently wandered in off the streets by mistake, shoved a sheet of paper across the desk.

"By signing up now, you can take advantage of our special. Six months of free classes." Her patronizing tone of voice implied that they were both aware Becca wouldn't last six months.

Christine Arness

A muscle-bound man in nylon shorts and a fishnet T-shirt wandered into the cubicle and attempted to wheedle a midnight movie date from the blond. Becca stared at the abbreviated class names on the page, too intimidated by the silent contempt for her flabbiness to ask for clarification.

"V'Ball" caught her eye and she seized it with the relief of a drowning victim spotting a life preserver floating nearby. The entry sparked memories of family picnics, friendly competition over a sagging net, grass tickling bare feet and fireworks after dark. She was aware, however, that her skills needed brushing up.

"Do you have a beginner's class in volleyball?"

The other woman didn't bother to glance in Becca's direction. "There's a sign-up sheet in the pink folder."

Becca located the folder in the pile stacked precariously on the corner of the desk and scribbled her name on the top sheet. The die was cast. She would breathe, eat and sleep volleyball until she had that perfect body.

The first session was scheduled for a week from Friday night. In an attempt to gain some confidence before hand, Becca resurrected a fitness DVD and gyrated faithfully each night while BoJangles purred in utter contentment on the couch. Ten hours of shopping finally yielded a peach short set that she felt made her thighs look miraculously thinner.

Inspired by memories of 4th of July family reunions, Becca also designed an advertising campaign for a local car dealership featuring children roasting marshmallows over a bonfire, families seated on blankets as dazzling fireworks exploded overhead and barefoot players hitting the volleyball over a net, their blissful expressions reflecting the twin joys of companionship and competition. Her boss and the client expressed delight with her concept with a bonus that would help pay for a year at The Fitness Studio.

Friday finally arrived—and found Becca on the expressway, struggling to fix a flat tire. Her elderly car intuitively seemed to know any plans she'd made to arrive early and somehow contrived to sabotage those good intentions. She was still scrubbing grease marks off her hands with a rag as she walked into The Fitness Studio.

Her blond guide perched on check-in duty at the desk tonight,

Perfect Body—Perfect Match

directing a scornful glance at the grease smears on Becca's peach shorts. Vowing she'd rather be lost in the desert for three days without water than ask the other woman for directions, Becca found a restroom and washed up before striking off on her own to locate the volleyball courts.

After interrupting a bizarre looking session that appeared as if it had something to do with either delivering babies or tummy-tightening, she found herself in the hall of an unexplored wing. Without warning, the double doors on the left burst open and someone erupted. Becca's first impression was of absolute male gorgeousness. Chestnut hair curled low on an intelligent forehead and the body beneath also appeared to be in excellent shape.

He froze, seemingly transfixed by the sight of the woman lurking in the hallway. Deciding an overlooked smear of grease might be responsible for his dazed condition, Becca put up her hand to cover her face and decided to clean up with more care before venturing out in public again.

When she turned to go, however, he waved an impatient hand. "You're late. Volleyball? B team, new player?"

B? B for beginner, of course. Before her head could finish the first nod, a sinewy arm shot out and caught Beeca in a bruising grip as the stranger marched her into a high-ceilinged room swarming with people clad in shorts and tennis shoes. Four separate nets were set up and the noise level was incredible.

Her captor shouted in her ear, "You're late, but it's a good thing you showed up at all."

"I had a flat tire—"

When he said "Wonderful!" in that hearty voice, she had the feeling he'd have said that even if she'd just announced she'd wiped out everyone in the building with an Uzi.

"What's your name?"

"Becca—"

"Nice to meet you, Becky," He continued, "We'd have had to forfeit with only five players and every game counts when we're getting so close to the playoffs. You missed warm-up so you'll just have to jump in cold." He hustled her across the gym floor to a huddle of two other men and two women.

"Everyone, this is Becky."

One of the guys grinned at her. "You're way too short to be on the front line. Zach, shall we run the 6-2 offense? Two setters? Hey, don't tell me you're a spiker."

Gazing up at his towering height, Becca didn't plan on telling him anything, She'd wandered into a land of giants. "I'm not exactly sure—"

"I'm Zach," the first guy interrupted. "We're up. Listen, we don't run a lot of quick sets, us guys prefer the hut/go. Charlie likes the pipe set while I'm always up for back row attacks. Watch out for those overpasses."

"Sure," she muttered, "if I knew what one looked like."

One of the other guys slapped her on the shoulder, leaving her arm number. "I'm Alex. When you're in the front, don't forget to call the numbers on the Spread O or X Series."

She nodded, but no one was paying attention to her. Dazed by the flow of incomprehensible instructions, Becca blinked at the volleyball in the hands of the man at her side. She didn't see any numbers.

There was a brief captains' meeting at the net. Things were moving too swiftly for a beginner's lesson. She crossed her fingers, hoping fervently that they'd split into smaller groups for instruction.

Idly, she admired the trimly muscled thighs visible beneath Zach's navy blue shorts, remembering how his eyes were almost a perfect match to the color of his outfit. As her gaze roved over the others present, she felt a sinking feeling in the pit of her stomach. Everyone else appeared to be bursting with athleticism, the type of obnoxiously fit people who, whenever conversation lags, might drop to the floor and do twenty push-ups.

Where were the uncoordinated architects, short-order cooks, dentists and art teachers seeking fun and relaxation? A man nearby picked up a ball and began slamming it against the wall, using his cupped hand to drive the volleyball forward. These people looked as though they should be marching behind their country's flag in the Olympics, not beginners at The Fitness Studio.

Zach's return interrupted her agitated thoughts.

"First serve!" he gloated. "Let's cream these guys and you," the navy blue gaze pierced Becca's soul, "relax and let us feast on their feeble attempts at blocking. We'll try to cover until you're into the flow."

Which wouldn't be for at least another ten years at least, Becca realized, but gamely followed her teammates. The girl in the server's position tossed the ball into the air and hammered it over the net, thus putting in motion the longest night of Becca's life.

Shocked, she heard a whistling sound as the ball screamed back over the net. Charlie popped it up to a girl, who, in turn, flicked the ball upwards for Zach's smashing spike.

Her teammates applauded the play enthusiastically, with Alex saying, "That was nearly a Six-Pack, Zach, he didn't see it coming."

Zach turned to her, those amazing eyes sparking with excitement. "What did I say? We'll cover for you and let you work into the play. Get ready for a storm, cause we're gonna bring the thunder!"

He faced the net again while Becca gulped in horror, struggling with the urge to run but judging from the velocity of the ball and eight teams playing simultaneously, she feared she'd never make it out alive.

She'd also never been much for storms. Shaking her head, Becca realized she had barely been able to follow the path of the volleyball, much less make a play on it. Once again she'd jumped into failure with both feet.

Without a doubt, she was out of her league. The inevitable moment of truth managed to be delayed, however, until the third serve of the match when the ball roared at Becca. She ducked.

"What's the matter? Afraid of the ball?" jeered one of the other girls, a brunette with a frosty eye and sturdy calves, crouching as the other team prepared to serve.

"You got that right," Becca muttered and gasped as the aforementioned object came whizzing at her again.

Zach immediately called time out and helped Becca up from her sprawled position on the floor. "Do I still have my ear?" she asked in plaintive tones.

Her teammates all groaned in unison and Zach winced. "You're not quite up to this level of play, are you?" he asked, his voice quiet amid the mutters from the others.

Becca could only offer a feeble smile If only she were Alice in

Wonderland and simply by eating a magic cake, she could shrink down to invisibility and escape the hostile glares of those around her.

Zach whirled and called the other team captain over for a conference. Becca stood apart from the others and watched as they discussed her fate.

"Either she plays or you forfeit." The man sent a malicious grin in Becca's direction as he spoke.

Zach spent a few minutes in futile argument before returning to his team. "You heard the verdict. They're going to hardnose it." He looked at Becca. "I know you lack the experience at this level of play, so are you going give it a try or shall we all go home? I warn you, it's very easy for an inexperienced player to get hurt. These guys and gals play rough."

Zach had taken the noble route, leaving the decision up to her. Becca gritted her teeth with determination. If she'd only stuck to one form of exercise instead of flitting around like a butterfly, she wouldn't be in this mess.

"I'll play," she announced with false bravado, adding under her breath, "Then I'll hunt down the woman who let me sign up to be a duck in a shooting gallery and ask for a refund."

The games were a nightmarish hail of volleyballs as big as basketballs with all serves and spikes aimed at Becca. She ducked and lunged while her teammates performed miraculous leaps and dives around her cringing form. Her only attempt at hitting the ball resulted in two painfully jammed fingers.

Sheer terror sent perspiration running down her face and plastered her tee-shirt against her torso. She knew the eye make-up she'd applied with such care must be a streaky mess. The hands of the huge clock on the wall crept while her own hands did their best to protect her from a Six-Pack, which she'd learned meant getting a volleyball spike in the face and had nothing to do with Zach's abdomen.

Zach stood the hero test, never once adding to the jeers or scowls aimed in her direction, doing his best to keep her from getting hit and deflecting the ball even though it often appeared out of his reach.

At last the ordeal ended. Stumbling off the court on shaky legs, Becca gathered from her teammates' comments as they changed shoes and packed up their gear that they had managed to win only one game.

Perfect Body—Perfect Match

No one said good-bye.

The women's locker room did not offer an escape from the hostile atmosphere. Becca stayed only long enough to wash the make-up from her face and winced at her reflection. Skin still blotchy from the combination of exercise and embarrassment, wisps of sweat soaked hair plastered to her face. Ugh! An inventory of her bruised hands also disclosed several broken fingernails. Wondering what other disaster could strike to end such a perfect evening, Becca shoved the locker room door open and into a solid object.

"Excuse me," she snapped to the man standing there and stalked off to locate a garbage disposal and shred her membership card.

He followed. "Wait a minute, please. It's Becca, not Becky, isn't it?"

She whirled to see Zach offering a sweet smile. *So he knows who you are. But folks also remember the Titanic and the Hindenburg*, she cautioned herself and nodded without stopping.

"Hey, Becca, wait up! I just wanted to tell you how much I admire your courage in playing. We'd have had to swallow every game as a loss if you'd left when you had the chance. We need every win to keep us in competition for our division."

Courage? Since when was ducking, quivering and sweating defined as bravery? Becca found herself smiling back. He really had the most gorgeous navy blue eyes ...

Fifteen minutes later found Becca and Zach in the juice bar of The Fitness Studio. Zach had selected a carrot and tomato swirl while Becca sipped a banana-apricot fizz.

Zach chuckled when he learned the meager extent of Becca's volleyball experience. "Despite everything, you showed promise," he assured her. "You stayed in the rotation and even tried to hit one or two. It'll just take a little proper instruction before you could play on a team."

Shuddering from the thought of even going near a volleyball court again, she balanced that terror against the fear of never seeing Zach again. "Proper instruction?"

"Proper private instruction." Zach grinned wickedly. "Our team needs an alternate. Why don't we discuss ways to get you up to speed over dinner on Sunday?"

Becca choked on the fizz in her drink. "Dinner?"

'Hey, I've still got to shower and change before they start turning off the lights and we've a lot left to talk about. As we haven't been properly introduced, I could bring references to my trustworthy character, if it would favorably influence your decision."

"People can be bribed to lie," Becca said with a smile.

"I'm great with mothers—you could introduce me to yours."

Beeca raised an eyebrow. "She's on a ten day cruise to Alaska."

Zach flicked a napkin across the table and it landed in Becca's lap. "New plan—if you want to play it cautious, we could meet at the restaurant."

They agreed to meet at the Doodlebug, which attempted to recreate the ambiance of the dance clubs of the 30's and 40's, complete with movie posters and a jukebox filled with vintage big band tunes.

Becca changed her mind about keeping the date on the average of ten times an hour over the next two days. Only the fact she'd failed to get his phone number kept her from cancelling.

As Becca entered the Doodlebug, her stomach flip-flopped with nerves. Three agonizing hours of standing in her walk-in closet had resulted in the choice of a pleated skirt and a pink flowered blouse.

Zach waited just inside the door, appropriately enough, under a poster for the movie, "Casablanca". The dark blue shirt under his sports jacket matched his amazing eyes. Becca made the snap judgment that she'd take Zach's warm smile over Humphrey Bogart's smoldering stare at Ingrid any day.

Even with reservations, they had a long wait but were finally seated near the raised dance floor. On the way to their table, Zach and Becca pointed out their favorite posters. Becca favored Fred and Ginger floating in each other's arms in "Top Hart", while Zach leaned toward "The Thin Man" with William Powell and Myrna Loy menaced by a trench coated figure. As they studied the posters for "42nd Street", "Gone with the Wind" and "Gaslight", the couples on the dance floor spun past to the toe-tapping beat of Benny Goodman.

Neither could resist the tantalizing rhythm of "Swing, Swing, Swing" when it blared from the jukebox. Zach held out his hand and Becca took it with confidence. Although clumsy on the volleyball court, she was at home on the dance floor and the two kept it up until their food arrived, whirling back to the table, breathless with laughter.

The waiter's frown seemed to indicate disapproval that they were more absorbed in each other than in the food served. As the conversation continued, they discovered common interests in black and white movies, photography and the St. Paul Saints baseball team.

Becca had never felt so at ease with and yet so attracted to a man. The little frown between his brows as he pondered a response had her struggling with the urge to reach out and smooth it away with her fingertips.

The question currently on the table was Becca's. "Do you believe the theory that people who enjoy black and white movies are escapists? Wanting to move back to a simpler, more uncomplicated time?"

The adorable frown appeared again. "No, I don't agree," Zach replied. "Many of the black and white films did address relevant social problems, such as child abuse, racial prejudice, poverty and war. Even though for the most part they featured happy endings, it doesn't make their points any less valid. It's only human to want everything to come up roses."

The waiter coughed apologetically as he presented the bill. "Excuse me, sir. I hate to interrupt, but there are other people who have reservations for this table."

Zach looked at his watch in disbelief. "We've been sitting here for nearly three hours!"

"There's a bridge over the stream behind the restaurant," the waiter, who apparently concealed a romantic soul under a bushy white moustache, offered in discreet whisper. "Perhaps a stroll in the moonlight would help settle the meal …"

Water murmured over the stones in the streambed as Zach and Becca walked out onto the wooden planks. The moon made its promised appearance from behind the clouds, casting shadows across Zach's rugged features and dappling the leaves of a nearby birch tree. Mallard ducks, connecting humans with bread crumbs, paddled gently below, craning their necks upward for the first hint of food.

Zach put his hands on Becca's arms and turned her to face him. As they gazed into each other's eyes, she wondered if Zach could hear her heart beating over the sound of the rushing water.

An impatient quack sounded from below. Zach grinned. "Keep your tail feathers on, fella," he murmured. "I'm going to kiss the lady."

The kiss and his embrace felt marvelously sweet, but Becca drew back. Things seemed to be moving too swiftly—new passions gripped her, tugged at her heart like the current below. She clutched the material of Zach's jacket for support, feeling the muscles in his arms tense at her touch.

He broke the spell, turning to lean on the railing of the bridge. "You overwhelm me, Becca. When I hold you, I can feel the breath in your body. I have the feeling that I want to hold you forever—let you live in my arms. They feel so empty without you."

Becca placed her hand on his shoulder. "I want to try that kiss again before committing myself," she whispered back.

Their lips met and the moon shivered in delight.

Only a heartbeat later, Zach glanced at his watch. "Do you realize it's nearly midnight? And as much as I hate to leave you, my alarm is going to ring in six hours."

"Let it ring. What about your empty arms?" Becca murmured, kissing his ear lobe.

He chuckled. "One more kiss, darling. One more to sustain me through the hard day's night."

Several kisses later, as he escorted Becca to her car, Zach brought up the reason for their first meeting. "Are you interested in a couple of volleyball lessons?"

She shook her head. "I've learned my lesson, thank you!"

He took her hand in a warm, possessive clasp. "Forget volleyball, but I want to see you again, Becca. You're so different from any other woman I've dated."

Different? Different as in chubby—out of shape? Images of the tanned and trim women who lived at the Fitness Studio shimmered before Becca's eyes. She yanked her hand free and slid behind the wheel, leaving the door and her options open.

"What's wrong, darling?" It would have taken a man with the hide of a rhinoceros not to feel the sudden chill.

She decided to be blunt. If honesty scared Zach off, she didn't want to pursue the relationship any further and she needed an answer. "Exactly why do you want to see me again? Let's face it, this is not the body of an athlete and it probably never will be. Why don't you go after the other women at the Fitness Studio—some pretty terrific bodies hang out there."

"Let's not complicate matters. I want to see you again because I'm attracted to you."

Becca looked down at the hands folded in her lap. Traitorous hands, aching to ruffle the smoothness of Zach's hair. "Thank you for dinner. I had a lovely time."

"Don't give me that 'lovely time' stuff! We had a definite spark going—if not a full-scale blaze. Look me in the eye and deny it if you can!"

He tilted up her chin in an abrupt movement, but his voice softened. "Becca, where did you get the idea I'd only be attracted by the outer wrappings? Hasn't the fact that we've talked non-stop for hours meant anything to you? I want more in a relationship than someone who works out three times a day and can beat me in arm wrestling whenever she feels like it."

Her look of disbelief goaded him on. "I'm thirty years old and it's time to get married and raise a family. I want to spend the rest of my life with a woman who can talk intelligently about world hunger, her career—anything but the number of laps she swims daily or her calorie count."

His impassioned response frightened Becca into taking refuge in flippancy. "Marriage? Aren't you're rushing things a little?"

"Perhaps, but I don't want your insecurities standing between us Haven't you felt the electricity? We fit—we generate the same excitement as the great screen couples, Bogart and Bacall, Gable and Lombard, Tracy and Hepburn …"

Becca couldn't help herself. "Laurel and Hardy?"

Zach's jaw dropped. Bowing his head into his hands, he slumped against the car, shaking with helpless laughter. "Need you ask what I see in you, Becca?" Sobering, he brushed a curl back from her cheek. "Give us a chance, please?"

The tender appeal in his voice melted the protective barrier of reserve she had kept between them. "I guess I don't know what I'm searching for in a relationship, Zach. Do you?"

"I want something spontaneous, one where our lives don't revolve around workouts and tanning booths. I want someone who can drop everything for a picnic in the country, laugh at a silly riddle or sit down with me and enjoy The Maltese Falcon without worrying about missing her aerobics class. I want to be part of a couple—a couple whose two parts make a perfect whole."

All of Becca's worries and theories about needing a great body to attract a great man had been left splintered on the pavement of the parking lot. This man, this gorgeous, thoughtful man, was telling her it was her inner self who mattered to him.

Bending to kiss her again, Zach said, "Let me tell you that I'm also a guy who appreciates beauty. Tonight I walked in the moonlight and kissed a beautiful woman. Moonlight becomes you, Becca. You're perfect, just the way you are. If a guy doesn't appreciate the real you, he's not worth trying to change yourself for him." His lips brushed her cheek. "Drive carefully, sweetheart."

Becca floated home about two inches above the driver's seat. Zach's words had freed her from the dragging weight of a poor self-image. The person who looked back at her in the rearview mirror and laughed had the sparkling eyes and flushed cheeks of a woman who knew she was beautiful.

The future seemed as bright as the moonlight silvering the pavement and somehow Becca knew Zach would be a part of that future.

Once inside her apartment, Becca realized she felt ravenously hungry. Had she managed to eat anything at dinner? Did the waiter ever bring any food? She hadn't noticed.

Lady BoJangles followed her out to the kitchen and watched with disapproval as Becca pulled a personal pan sized pizza from the freezer and put it in the microwave.

The cat meowed and Becca chuckled at her pet's attitude. "Don't worry, Lady Bo," she assured her. "It's going to take a lot of nourishment to keep my figure at its current level of perfection."

THE END

Flutter of Wings

"No." My sister's voice was firm. "Drag me to the beach without sunblock, use a harsh cleanser on my bathroom sink, or buy me a ticket for a punk rock concert—no matter what the torture, I won't throw you a party."

"But, Linda, my apartment isn't big enough to even play double-handed solitaire! I'll scrub your kitchen floor and baby-sit for a month—all you have to do is loan me the grill and your backyard." I am not above groveling for a good cause.

My sister shifted in her chair. In her eighth month of pregnancy, she was somewhat sensitive about references to beached whales. "And," Linda announced, "I refuse to wear an apron that says 'Kiss the Cook.'"

"I'll handle every detail." I played my trump card. "I need to find a way to get Sam into an unpressured social setting."

"A man's involved?" Linda stretched out her legs as if to check whether she could still see her toes. "Where did you meet him?"

"My current night class. Sam and I go out for coffee every Thursday after class."

My sister sets me up with each eligible man who strays into her orbit, and I could tell she had mixed emotions about my mention of Sam: delight at the prospect of a possible wedding in my future and disappointment that she had nothing to do with it.

But she gave in with a graceful nod. "All right. I'll loan you the backyard, if you'll babysit and help clean the house."

"Thanks." I blew her a kiss and headed for the door. "Sam and Gail seem perfect for each other."

"Lori! I thought you and Sam …"

"I'm still waiting on the Lord, Linda."

"Waiting on the Lord means being sensitive to God's leading. News flash! When the right man enters your life, don't expect bells, sirens, whistles, or the Angel Gabriel to appear and say, 'Hey, here's the guy for you…'"

"Since God created me, He knows I'm often oblivious to what's right under my nose, and He'll have to send a special messenger. Any angel will do if Gabriel's busy." I patted Linda's shoulder and she stuck out her tongue at me. "Anyway, I happened to mention Sam to Gail and she wants to meet him."

"I didn't know Gail was such a close friend of yours."

"She's an acquaintance, but I can still do her a favor. You're not the only matchmaker in the family." I made my escape before she could retract permission for the party.

After our next class, I told Sam that the preparations for Saturday's barbecue were progressing. "I still need to scour the grill and help clean house. All you have to do is show up and be charming."

"And you think I'll like Gail." His smile seemed somehow lopsided.

"She's bright, witty, and gorgeous. What's not to like?"

He stirred his coffee, his expression thoughtful. "Gail sounds perfect. But will she be perfect for me?"

I thought I detected an odd note of reluctance in his voice. I smiled. Sam deserved the best. "You'll get along like toast and jam."

"As good as we do?" He chuckled, and I thought smugly that Gail couldn't help but be enchanted by this man.

When I called Gail to assure her Sam was coming, she tried to pump me for personal details, but other than describing him as nice looking and friendly, I was at a loss.

Sam and I don't discuss superfluous issues like net income or careers. Instead, we conduct intense debates about social problems and our favorite old movies. We talk about the importance of seeking God's direction in our lives and share our dreams for the future. I'd never asked him if he belonged to a health club or whether he had great benefits at work.

Although dissatisfied with my crumbs of information, Gail vowed to

Flutter of Wings

give me her firstborn child if this relationship made it to the altar and said she'd see me on Saturday.

Novice that I was at nurturing the tender sprouts of romance, I began to dread the barbecue. What if Sam and Gail took one look at each other and decided that they preferred English muffins and peanut butter?

After a frenzied morning spent rounding up tricycles from the latest demotion derby in the back yard and fixing salads, my hair looked like I'd been tumbled in the dryer.

"Don't blame me," Linda chirped as I wiped strained carrots off the kitchen floor. "I warned you my youngest was in the food-throwing stage." She patted her rounded tummy covered in yellow cotton. "How do I look?"

My own stomach felt as if someone had set up an abacus inside and was sliding beads across the strings with vicious thrusts. "Like a straw with a beach ball in it."

By the time the guests arrived, we were speaking again, and the back yard soon sizzled with the scent of grilling meat and the sound of lively conversation.

Gail drifted up. "Where's Sam?"

I shaded my eyes with a loaf of French bread. "Guess he's fashionably late."

She showed her perfect teeth in a barracuda smile. "I turned down a tennis match with a CPA to meet this man, Lori. You'd better deliver."

Leaving the 'or else' part of the threat unuttered, she moved over to sample the dip. Regretting that I'd gone to so much trouble for someone as congenial as a case of hives, I placed the bread on the buffet table.

Turning, I saw my sister deep in conversation with a man on crutches, his left leg in a cast from the knee down, and I hurried over.

"Sam, what did you do to yourself?" I demanded, horrified. "You were fine on Wednesday!"

Snatching a child from under the wheels of a speeding car or slipping on the deck of one's yacht were equally acceptable answers, but Sam looked sheepish. "Fell down the steps at the track on Friday morning. I'm having a little trouble getting around."

Gail, who'd trailed over after me, sucked in her breath. I remembered her partiality for briefcases, sports cars, and pension plans and launched a missile glare that said "be nice" in her direction.

My sister smiled. I distrusted that smile.

After the standard introductions, Linda chirped, "We were talking about Sam's job—it sounds so fascinating. Tell Gail what you do for a living, Sam."

I wished this subject had been raised later than sooner, after Sam and Gail had had a chance to get to know one another. From his assured manner, I'd assumed Sam held a position in the business world, but we'd never gotten down to specifics.

"I guess you'd say I'm a mechanic."

My heart sank. A blue-collar guy would clash with Gail's rapidly purpling features. Linda, always helpful, shoved a bowl of olives under Gail's nose as if they were smelling salts.

"Thanks for setting me up with a grease monkey in need of Gamblers Anonymous." Snatching an olive, Gail turned away. No firstborn child for me.

Attempting to gloss over her rudeness, I took Sam's arm and steered him toward the buffet. "Hint: avoid the fruit salad. A few of my fingertips might be mixed in with the melon slices."

He chuckled, a warm, rich sound that always made me smile.

Handicapped by the crutches, Sam indicted his selections, and I filled his plate. While he began the awkward task of maneuvering his injured leg under the picnic table, I went back for my own food and our drinks.

As I set a glass of lemonade by his plate, he said with a shrewd glance in my direction, "So, that was Gail."

My cheeks flamed as hot as the grill. "I'm sorry it didn't work out. You're sweet and have a great sense of humor. She just didn't hang around long enough to find out all your great qualities."

"But you've certainly done that." He toyed with a forkful of potato salad. "Since Gail doesn't want me, how about you?"

I spilled coleslaw in my lap and took a hasty sip of lemonade to clear my whirling head. Scraping cabbage off my shorts, I recognized what had been staring me in the face all along. Sam was a man I found very attractive. And I'd tried to fix him up with Gail! Obviously, the damage to the ozone layer was having a dangerous effect on my brain.

Flutter of Wings

Sam continued with a smile. "I didn't come to meet Gail today. I came to be with you. Does the idea of my working with my hands bother you, Lori?"

He held out his calloused hands, hands that courteously pulled out my chair at the coffee shop on Thursday evenings and gestured so eloquently when he talked.

Remembering his crooked smile the night I'd babbled on about Gail's qualities, I realized he'd been indicating an interest in me all along, but I'd been too caught up in my own plans to notice.

I recalled something else. "Remember the first time we went out for coffee? You changed a flat tire for a pregnant woman in the parking lot. Everyone else walked by, but you stopped. That incident made me think of the story of the good Samaritan. I think your hands are beautiful, my good Samaritan, and as long as you wash them before meals, I don't care if you feed lions at the zoo."

Those beautiful hands reached out to encompass my fingers, sticky shreds of cabbage and all. "I have a confession to make, Lori. When I brought my nephew in to register for college and heard your bubbling laugh, it was as if God grabbed me by the shoulder and said, 'Hey, that's the woman for you!' I decided to sign myself up for the same class that you did—whether it was folk dancing or ceramics."

Unprepared for such frankness, I tried to pass his words off with a joke. "It's a good thing you didn't hit it off with Gail. Because if you had, then I'd have had the job of breaking you two up after going through all this trouble to throw you together."

Sam smiled, looking over my shoulder, and I turned to see my sister bouncing merrily between knots of people scattered throughout her backyard.

"To be honest, I didn't want to hit it off with Gail—that's why your sister brought up my job right away."

"That was Linda's idea?" I bit my lip and decided to apologize again for that crack about the beach ball.

"And as long as I'm confessing, although I work with engines and I still consider myself a grease monkey at heart, I actually spend quite a bit of time at the office since I invented something that improves the fuel economy in race cars. Now I have my own corporation, and during the racing season, I spend a lot of time flying around the country to research and make adjustments that help the top drivers keep their edge."

"Corporation?" I gulped.

"You're spooning fruit salad into your lemonade, Lori."

I looked down. So I was. "But, Sam…!"

He winked at me. His eyes were a warm brown, with dazzling flecks of gold, tiny reflections of the sun. "I promise I'll wash my hands before leaving the office. So, any more questions?"

Dazed, I shook my head. My career as a matchmaker was over before it ever started. I had reached the pinnacle of the profession, having fixed myself up with the perfect man, even though Linda had been the first to recognize my interest in Sam was personal.

Imagine my own sister, a special messenger from God! I grinned as she gleefully flashed me the "OK" sign.

She wasn't Gabriel, but when she hurried past, I thought I heard the flutter of wings.

THE END

When Hearts Collide

The sound of breaking glass was actually the shattering of a pleasant fantasy, but at the time Katie was aware only that she was involved in her first auto accident.

Shaken by the impact of the collision between the Camero and her elderly Mustang, she squinted apprehensively through the dazzling glare of the sun on her windshield at the other vehicle.

Moments before, the driver of the Camero had his hand upraised in casual greeting. Horror swiftly replaced the smile with a look of shocked disbelief as he realized her Mustang wasn't going to stop. Unfortunately, Katie's frantic spinning of the wheel as her brakes refused to hold coincided with the other car's evasive action.

Echoes of the crash still ringing in her ears, Katie unfastened her seat belt with shaking fingers, climbed out of the low-slung bucket seat and wobbled forward. After two steps, she had to lean against her car's fender for support; the ground seemed to be heaving beneath her feet.

Was it an earthquake to add fresh devastation? No, she was trapped in a blast of words seeking to whirl her away, like an old newspaper caught in a windstorm. Now she knew why they now named hurricanes after men? Surely, nothing could match the masculine fury now raging around her.

"What's the matter with you? Didn't you see the stop sign? Or was your Seeing Eye dog taking a nap in the back seat?

His sarcastic tone glittered as brightly as the mingled shards of broken glass from the headlights of both vehicles. Katie shook her head to clear it.

She knew this man. Despite the scowl, his face was as familiar as her reflection in the mirror when she brushed her teeth. Each morning they passed on their opposite ways and he saluted her with a wave and a smile. His handsome features reminded her of a poster depicting Sleeping Beauty being kissed awake by a prince, a prince whose heart-stopping smile had decorated her room until she was fourteen.

As the other driver surveyed the twisted nose of his vintage Camero, he shuddered with revulsion and turned on Katie. She hugged the battered side of her car for support as he raised his voice to a shout.

"You've ruined her!"

Katie felt tangled in the sticky web of a nightmare, the chilling kind where monsters stalked innocent children playing in a field of daisies. Perhaps she'd hit her head on the steering wheel. Perhaps she was still asleep and in an hour would be waving a greeting to the man in the baby blue Camero.

As he pounded the hood of her crumpled car with a clenched fist and vented his frustration, Katie remembered the hours she'd spent visualizing their first meeting. They would pass on the street and he would stop, studying her features with interest. "Say, don't I know you? You're that pretty girl who waves to me each morning!" Coffee, an intimate candlelight dinner, dancing—"Katie, you're so special, darling"—then marriage, children and happily ever after.

The prince, whose smiles she'd cherished and hugged deep inside, the man whose every gesture had been stored away as a special memory, had been changed by enchantment into a fire-breathing dragon.

A crowd composed of dog walkers, joggers and the curious occupants of neighboring houses gathered to view and comment on the accident. Cars trapped behind the two stalled vehicles honked impatiently.

The sun burned down on Katie's uncovered head. She was dizzy and her lower lip, bitten through on impact, felt as if it had swelled to the size of her mother's strawberry pin cushion.

The edges of the scene seemed fuzzy and surrealistic. She longed to escape and lie down with a cool cloth over her eyes, but the prince-dragon was still demanding an explanation.

She swallowed a giggle. You could almost see the puffs of smoke emerging from his nostrils as he snorted and snarled.

"Get a grip on yourself, Katie, my girl. I think you're delirious," she cautioned herself before saying aloud, "I'm very sorry but it was an accident. My brakes must have failed. I tried to avoid you but we seemed to have been on the same wave length."

He winced at the word "wave" and swept an accusing hand at the damage. "Do you think being sorry is going to fix *that*?"

"And do you expect me to wave—oops, I apologize, poor choice of words—point a magic wand and have your car restored? I'm insured, so relax."

If this had been a story book romance, he would be cuddling her shocked, trembling body against his powerful chest, their hearts beating as one while he assured her he would take care of everything.

Well, this wasn't a romance, this was reality and the man of her dreams seemed unmoved at the sight of the blood she could feel trickling down her chin. Since he continued to abuse both her and her poor battered car, her Irish temper finally sparked. Katie stalked over and slammed her own hand down on the hood of the his Camero with each word for emphasis. "I'm sorry—I'm insured—Stop shouting!"

He did, abruptly switching to a moan of pure pain that she had dared to lay hands on his injured sweetheart. The pathetic tinkle of the last glass fragments parting from the headlight casing and falling to the street almost brought him to his knees.

"She's only fit to be scrapped. This was a sleek, hot-blooded cruising animal until your junk heap mauled her!"

As she stared into his hate-filled eyes, Katie wondered what she could do to strike back. Kick a tire? She didn't want the situation degenerating any further into a black and white slapstick routine as two motorists methodically dismantle each other's cars in revenge.

"Calm down, mister. She still looks like an animal. Instead of a thoroughbred, though, you've got a bull dog."

The crowd tittered in appreciation of Kate's wit, but the driver of the other car clenched his fists and stalked towards her. She felt a tremor of fear at having pushed him too hard. A male jury would never convict him. A shrill cry from the growing throng of onlookers stopped him from committing justifiable homicide.

"Adam, that that you? Remember, you've a court appearance at ten this morning—oh, Adam, your car! How dreadful!"

The woman who approached was apparently also a lawyer. A calfskin briefcase swung at her side and the severely tailored black suit did nothing to detract from her ash blond femininity. Slipping a comforting hand through her colleague's rigid arm, she turned a laser-blue gaze on Katie.

"What happened here? Are you hurt, Adam?"

"She destroyed my car, Michelle! My baby's ruined. She'll never be the same. This woman ran right through a stop sign and plowed into me!"

"Adam, what a terrible tragedy! I can empathize—I know the pain you're experiencing. I'd be just as devastated if a vandal destroyed one of my Persian rugs."

He scowled, as if resenting any comparison between his car and a carpet.

Katie felt very tired. Adam and Michelle deserved each other. She hoped they would get married and buy a Great Dane which refused to be housebroken around Michelle's Persian rugs and chewed the upholstery in Adam's next car.

Since Adam seemed wrapped up in his own personal torment, Katie offered Michelle an explanation. "As I told Adam before, I'm insured and it was truly an accident. My brakes failed. I'm very sorry."

Michelle paid as much attention as if a slimy bug had crawled out of a crack in the sidewalk and attempted to address her. After a haughty glance in Katie's general direction, Michelle patted Adam on the shoulder in an attempt to offer comfort.

Adam, however, was still obsessed with his grievance. "Don't ever wave at me again!" he snapped petulantly and turned his back on Katie.

"Wave?" Michelle arched perfectly plucked brows. "You know each other?"

Her assessing glance swept over Katie's buttercup yellow sun dress, so bright and cheery an hour early, now smudged with dust from leaning on the car, the puffed and bloodied lip she'd seen in her rearview mirror.

When Hearts Collide

Michelle smiled.

The contemptuous smile hurt Katie more than the sting of her cut mouth. To keep the tears from spilling over, she turned to survey the damage to her Mustang. The front of her car was badly crumpled and the jagged metal had also cut and collapsed a tire. The effect was that of a dignified matron with a bloody nose.

She wished fervently that the police would arrive and issue her a ticket—or arrest her. Jail would be better than being imprisoned here in the street with Adam and Michelle.

"Katie?"

The familiar voice sent her spinning around, searching for a friendly face in a haze of hostility. "Matthew! I'm so glad to see you!"

Puzzled by the warmth of her greeting, the man thus addressed sent a quick glance over his shoulder, as if to check whether another Matthew had wandered into the vicinity.

Katie's relief was genuine, although their acquaintance was limited to a lunch date several weeks ago. Matthew had installed the new computer system in Katie's office. She'd enjoyed the conversation, but the memory of a gleaming smile, wavy chestnut hair and a baby blue Camero had kept her from accepting a second date.

Now the concern in his voice as he asked if she was all right sent the tears she'd been too proud to shed coursing down her cheeks. "My brakes didn't work—I turned his vintage car into a bull dog—he keeps going on and on about the damage until I could scream! I apologized, Matthew, but he yelled at me." She gulped. "And she smiled …"

Within minutes, Matthew had Katie seated inside his truck while he procured a plastic bag filled with crushed ice from a neighboring residence for her swollen lip.

When a policeman finally appeared, Matthew explained about the brake failure and insisted that Katie be interviewed as briefly as possible. A sullen Adam watched his bruised vintage baby hauled away by a tow truck before climbing into Michelle's BMW.

Matthew opened the door. "I'm afraid your car isn't drivable, Katie, so I called the garage down the street for a tow truck. I'm going to run you over to the ER for a check-up and stitches in that lip. I don't like the way it's bleeding."

"I'm not too crazy about it myself," Katie quipped feebly behind the makeshift ice bag. "But don't you have to be somewhere on a job?"

Matthew's gentle smile widened and he winked. "I'll call in that I have an emergency. Can't abandon a lady in distress, can I?"

As he went around to the driver's side and climbed up behind the wheel, Katie studied him out of the corner of her eye. Why had she decided this friendship wouldn't be worth developing? Because Matthew wore khaki work pants instead of a three piece suit? Carried a tool box instead of a briefcase? Went to night school instead of joining the country club?

Just because his features weren't poster perfect didn't mean he wouldn't be perfect for Katie O'Brien. After the trauma of the morning, Katie was ready to discard her silly, insubstantial fantasies about a knight in shining armor for a man who could chase away the real life dragons that lurked around every corner.

As Matthew turned the key in the ignition, Katie reached over and patted his hand.

He glanced at her. "Feel all right, Katie?"

"I'm glad you rode your white charger today, Matt."

"Charger? This is a Chevy truck—not a Dodge Charger. Are you sure you're not concussed?"

Katie leaned her throbbing head back and sighed contentedly. "I may not be an automotive expert, Matt, but I do know my knights."

THE END

At Home to Roost

"Linen napkins?" Pulling on his sweater, Peter gave his wife a puzzled look.

"I want everything to be just perfect," Rosemary said, folding the last one and smoothing the tablecloth.

Peter chuckled. "We never used cloth napkins at breakfast when the girls lived at home."

"This Easter is the first holiday everyone is able to be with us," Rosemary reminded him. "We're going to show all the family in-laws that gracious living is possible away from the city."

Buttoning his jacket, Peter kissed her on the cheek and headed out to do chores. As she bustled around the kitchen, Rosemary thought back …

She and Peter had been blessed with three daughters. The girls had loved farm life, each participating in 4-H and showing livestock.

Both had fallen in love while away at college, Dorrie with an aspiring physician, Karla with a software developer and Alyson with an accountant. Naturally, Rosemary and Peter had hoped that at least one child would marry a man who'd be willing to take over the farm eventually. That wish hadn't been fulfilled, however, they both knew their daughters' happiness came first.

Now, the girls and their families lived in different cities, and opportunities for reunions were few and far between. Their husbands were always cordial, but Rosemary didn't know them well enough to be truly comfortable in their company.

Everybody had arrived last night. This morning, Rosemary was determined to overwhelm them with country-style hospitality. There'd be omelets for the adults, and French toast strips and maple syrup for the three little ones. A succulent ham awaited its turn in the oven for the noon meal.

Peter strode in from chores, ice glittering on his shoulders. "Getting slick out—it's still sleeting."

"How are the new chicks?" Rosemary asked, feeling a twinge of concern.

"All fifty are still alive and peeping. They'll be okay … *if* the power stays on."

Hurrying to finish breakfast preparations while Peter cleaned up, Rosemary scowled at the gloomy sky outside.

Dorrie strolled into the kitchen with her husband and two children. Alyson and her husband and Karla and Matt and the baby soon came downstairs to join them. Rosemary scurried around her warm, wonderful smelling kitchen, so happy to have the girls home yet still unsure what to say to her sons-in-law. None of them had a country background and she felt awkward in attempting to initiate any conversation.

She was adding bacon to the omelet mixture when the lights flickered and went out.

Rosemary tried her best to smile. "Ice on the lines," she said. Turning to her daughters, she advised. "You better put sweaters on the kids."

Alyson jumped up. "I'll get the wood stove started. Everything will be fine."

Shaking her head, Rosemary thought about the newly hatched babies in the chicken house. Without the heat lamps on, they'd quickly freeze to death.

Peter appeared, reached for his coat … and hesitated. Rosemary realized her husband wasn't going to suggest the only method of saving the chicks. He knew how much the reunion and all her careful planning meant to her.

Then she recalled the wisdom her mother had shared on their wedding day, advice that had come in handy more than once during nearly thirty years of marriage: "Remember, dear, you're not only marrying a farmer, you're also marrying the land and the livestock. Always think of it as a package deal."

Case In Point

Rosemary nodded to Peter, and then grinned at the grandchildren. "Guess what?" she announced. "We're having 'company' for breakfast!"

The omelets ended up as a big casserole cooked on top of the wood stove. The grandchildren helped their mothers toast bread in the family room fireplace.

That adventure, however, was nothing compared with the excitement of watching fifty peeping yellow balls of fluff peck at feed in a makeshift pen in the kitchen!

Warm and well fed, the curious chicks were soon hopping over improvised barriers to make a break for freedom. The grandchildren shrieked in glee with each attempted escape. Even Rosemary chuckled when Alyson's husband sprawled on his belly to recapture a fugitive behind the refrigerator.

When the power had been finally restored, and order along with it, the ice had been completely broken ... both outside the sprawling farmhouse and within. Easter dinner—a little later than planned—was accompanied by happy chatter and lots of laughter.

Afterward, as Rosemary surveyed the newly scrubbed kitchen floor, Peter put a hand on her shoulder. "Satisfied, honey? I know things didn't turn out quite like you planned."

She leaned against her husband and sighed. "Mother used to say that children, like chickens, always come home to roost. But, *next* Easter, let's hope only chocolate bunnies provide the excitement!"

THE END

Harvest Gold

Theresa zipped up Megan's jacket and planted a kiss on the furrowed brow of her youngest child. "No more frowns! Tomorrow's Saturday and you can help Daddy all day. Hurry, sweetie, or you'll miss the bus."

Jerry and Amy trooped into the kitchen and picked up their lunches. At the door, they turned to give her an appealing look, both barrels.

Although her heart ached for them, Theresa shook her head. "I know you love harvest season, but you've got to go to school."

Through the window, she watched them walk to the gate in their new clothes. No hand-me-downs left to pass from Amy to Megan. New shoes, new jackets. Glancing around the room, she felt again an unpleasant tingle of shock at its unfamiliarity.

Theresa was loading the dishwasher when Bruce strode in. She smiled at her husband. "How goes the harvest?"

"Great! Gorgeous fall day, hon. Make sure you spend some time outside enjoying that high blue sky."

After washing his hands, he poured himself a cup of coffee. "All that water pressure still makes me jump—I'm not used to living in such luxury." Looking around, he took a sip. 'You must be in seventh heaven. All the stove burners work, the refrigerator spits out ice at the touch of a button—"

Theresa felt a surge of irritation at her husband's blindness. "But this morning I mixed up our pancakes in a stainless steel bowl instead of using Grandmother Evelyn's spatterware. I'm surrounded by things bought from a store, objects without history. He could God do this to us?"

Bruce's wind-reddened face creased in concern. "Honey, we agreed that the most important thing is that we all survived unhurt. We should be thankful, not angry."

"Alive, but without a past." Theresa added soap and slammed the dishwasher door. "Family photo albums from three generations, Grandpa's love letters to Grandmother while he was in Europe during the war—all ashes!"

"We're alive," Bruce repeated and gave her a patient smile. "What if the fire had started while we were asleep in our beds instead of safe at church? I know your grandmother's things meant the world to you, but she'd be the first to say that they weigh pretty light on the scale compared to Jerry, Amy, and Megan. The kids need us to be strong, Tee. Remember, they're going through a difficult time, too."

Long after Bruce had gone back out to the fields, Theresa sat and brooded. Although thankful that they'd been protected from physical harm, she still felt an aching sense of loss. The oak harvester table would seem like an alien in this spanking new kitchen, but she missed its beautiful wood grain. Bruce didn't understand the importance of heirlooms or how much she had cherished the tangible evidence of the unbroken cords which created a family.

Gathering laundry in their bedroom, Theresa kept her eyes averted from the space where her grandmother's quilt rack should be standing. Grandmother had designed the "Golden Harvest" pattern quilt featuring delicate sprays of wheat on a cream and blue background for Theresa's wedding.

Her heart a stone in her breast, Theresa lugged a basket filled with wet towels out to the clothesline strung in the back yard. The scarred wooden poles had somehow escaped the fiery holocaust which had consumed both the house and her past. As she worked, Theresa tried to count her blessings but her thoughts kept straying to her losses.

As the towels danced, she recalled her grandmother's wedding toast. "You name means 'reaper', Theresa. God's blessed you with a family that has truly sown the seeds of love. Now you and your children will reap the benefits. Always treasure the fruits of the harvest."

Christine Arness

But that harvest was gone, reduced to charred timbers and soot. After her parents' death in an automobile accident, Theresa had gone to live with her grandparents, with Evelyn serving as both mother and grandmother. Tears gathered in Theresa's eyes as she touched the only heirloom left to pass on to her own children, Evelyn's wedding ring. The band seemed almost paper thin and too large for her finger, but she treasured this last remaining link to her beloved grandmother.

Caught up in her unhappy reflections, Theresa reached down for another towel, only to discover that the basket was empty. Stretching, she looked around and decided Bruce was right—the day was too beautiful to be spent indoors. She wandered out to this barnyard where a wagonload of soybeans sat untended and suddenly remembered being a little girl on her grandfather's farm.

Impulse quickly turned into action and soon she sat perched on a shifting pile of beans. Running her fingers through them, she recalled a childish fantasy that the beans were jewels.

"I'm a princess," Theresa said aloud. "I'm very, very rich. I live in a castle and can buy anything I want!"

But the glow of pleasure faded almost instantly. A barnful of gold coins couldn't buy back her grandmother's dishes or the lovingly stitched Golden Harvest quilt. No amount of riches could bring her parents and grandparents back to life.

In a silent cry, she asked, *God, how could you do this to me?*

Wiping away a tear, Theresa froze, staring at her hand. The ring was gone!

She knew the precious band must have slid from her finger while she sifted through the beans. Whispering frantic prayers for assistance, Theresa scrabbled through the soybeans, although she knew her quest was as hopeless as searching for a needle in the proverbial haystack. As if mocking her anxiety, the beans slipped merrily through her clawing fingers.

Weeping, she gave up. "Grandma!" she cried aloud. "I've failed you! Everything's lost. If you were here, you'd say—"

Theresa stopped in mid-sob, realizing exactly what her grandmother would say to such blatant self-pity. "Bosh and nonsense, Theresa!

Harvest Gold

You've got a loving husband, three healthy children, and a new house filled with fancy appliances and you're bawling like a baby?"

"But a house isn't a home, Grandma," she whispered. "You were the one who taught me that money can't buy happiness."

Eyes closed, Theresa tried to imagine what her grandma would say to that. Probably something along the lines of "Making a house into a home is your job, Theresa. Doesn't the Good Book say that before the reaper, comes the sower? You've got fertile ground, child. Start sowing!"

Someone, Theresa realized, needed to plant the happy memory seeds. With careful nurturing, love would sprout and grow strong enough to withstand life's droughts and storms. She sat stunned, glimpsing for the first time the glory of her grandmother's true legacy, a gift which could never be lost, stolen, or destroyed.

She scrambled out of the wagon and ran toward the house, her heart soaring like a kite riding the wind. No more tears of self-pity. She'd fix a special supper and tonight they'd have an hour of family storytelling before bedtime. Plans for a new quilt were forming in her head. She'd call it "Loving Harvest" and make one for each of her children.

Theresa paused to pat a passing barn cat. "Every tradition," she told it excitedly, "has to start somewhere!"

THE END

Case in Point

The woman's head was bent, a silken shower of hair concealing her features. Only the rigid set of the jaw was visible, a hint of pale lips pressed together. The fingers of her right hand nervously twisted an engagement ring, as though to wrench the sparkling stone from its setting.

I smothered a growing feeling of discouragement. The woman seated across the desk had retreated behind an aloof curtain of privacy, shutting out the unpleasantness of our meeting with the effectiveness of a soundproof wall.

In an effort to regain my client's attention, I rustled the papers lying under my fingertips and leaned forward compellingly.

"Your husband's attorney is going to have some very personal questions for you on the stand, Dorothea. Are you prepared to answer them?"

"I feel so shaky, Allyson. Is there any way we could postpone this?" Dorothea Chapin evaded, meeting my gaze for a brief moment before glancing away.

"It's already been continued twice." I endeavored to speak with restraint, but a tension headache had begun to massage my temples with painful fingers. The woman was impossible! "You're the one who filed for divorce. At some point, you're going to have to face the music."

She murmured an inaudibly fretful reply and pleated her handkerchief with coral-tipped fingers. I watched with fascinated interest, expecting the fragile material to tear at any moment.

Case in Point

It held and I returned to the list of points enumerated on the legal pad lying on the desk. Locating the last item, I placed my finger on it for emphasis. "Now as to the question of maintenance, would you be willing to agree to split the difference in our proposals?"

The verbal fencing continued. Mrs. Chapin was adept at keeping up her guard while I tried to extract answers of more than one syllable, probing beneath the defensive shell of apathy for a concrete basis with which to work.

Under questioning, she insisted she currently had no intention of compromising on the maintenance issue. She deserved every penny she was demanding; she wanted him to suffer.

In the next breath, however, there was a faint murmur of worry over her husband's back problem. His health insurance didn't cover the necessary therapy twice a week. I ignored this interjection for the defense and continued to mine for nuggets of information.

Domestic violence? No, he'd never struck her. He wasn't even the type to raise his voice when upset. Mr. Chapin had the annoying tendency of retreating to his office at the college whenever tension hovered over the household. At least that was where she thought he was hiding. It was impossible to verify, but she had her suspicions about a bleached blond majoring in English…

Despite the concentration on the task at hand, I found a fragment of my attention straying to the case as a whole. Heart-wrenching divorces seemed to be the rule lately and not the exception.

Mrs. Chapin was the newest member of my divorce clientele. Although fashionably attired, her make-up had been applied with shaking hands and the pallor of her features was accentuated by violet shadows under the eyes. A dazed expression hinted of many sleepless nights.

I tried in vain to conceal my exasperation. Dorothea's passive refusal to assist in clarifying her desires with regard to settlement had been the biggest stumbling block to negotiations in this case.

Dorothea Chapin remained motionless in her chair, only the restless hands betraying her inner turmoil. Some women reacted to the stress of divorce proceedings by retreating into themselves, wrapping gossamer illusions around their delicate psyches and avoiding situations that would force them into making a decision. Others tried to overcome the strain with bright chatter, strewing meaningless smiles and empty gestures during their interviews.

Several of my clients had managed to deal with the stress in a calm, positive manner, but Dorothea Chapin lacked the necessary emotional fiber. Pain gleamed through the chinks of her poise, giving the appearance of a porcelain doll who had been dropped, its perfect features slightly cracked, damaged beyond repair.

I checked my watch with a sigh. We had been shut into my closet-sized office for over an hour and it was difficult to judge how much of my patient briefing had filtered through the numbing fog of Dorothea's exhaustion. Pen in hand, I ran a final check for any points which had not been covered, successfully concealing apprehension about my pupil's performance. Like a doctor or nurse, one struggled to avoid becoming emotionally involved with the sufferer. Divorce cases were similar to treating a critically ill patient, the cure sometimes beyond my skill.

Gathering up my papers and Surface computer, I slid them back into a fawn shaded briefcase with the gold clasp. The briefcase had been a birthday gift from Andrew… With an effort, I wrenched my thoughts from straying down that tantalizing footpath and rose.

"Please remember not to bring up suspicions about your husband's infidelity. Your petition is not based on the grounds of adultery. Try to stay calm under questioning and keep your answers brief. Look at me if you need any coaching. Don't make Judge Merrick strain to hear you. He becomes irritable if he has to continually ask a witness to repeat herself."

Mrs. Chapin stood up in response to my crisp gesture toward the door. I had learned the hard way that sympathy would only start her crying again. The smooth patina of the oaken desk was streaked with fingermarks and two tiny dots of moisture, indicated that several tears had escaped the fumbling stabs of the handkerchief.

The desk had been a witness to many sobbing confidences over the last few weeks. The sharp increase in the percentage of tearful sessions among my clientele was discouraging. Where were all of the calm, everything-laid-out-on-the-table-and-agreed-to divorces my colleagues talked about? Divorces were an easy way to earn a good fee, an older lawyer had informed me just the other day over lunch. Get an adequate retainer, prepare the papers, one trip to the courthouse and it was all over. No heartbroken sobs, no midnight calls from women whose lives were crumbling around them, no children made frantic by the prospective loss of a parent or by the necessity of having to choose between Mommy or Daddy ...

The courthouse was only five blocks from the office and I elected to cover the distance on foot. Perhaps a brisk walk in the winter air would bring a little color to my client's cheeks and orientate the distraught woman to her surroundings.

Dissolution of Marriage. The phrase wrapped in tissue paper the old-fashioned stigma of the word 'divorce'. I sometimes wondered about the meaning behind the words. What was being dissolved? The bonds of matrimony? A personal relationship? Could this be accomplished merely by obtaining a piece of paper signed by a judge? From the high percentage of post-decree cases, it seemed to be just the beginning of a nightmare for most women.

Dorothea carefully placed one foot in front of the other, a gliding automaton. Did the downcast eyes note the wind-nipped faces of the passers-by, the colorful panorama of the traffic on the street and sidewalks? Shoppers laden with packages and bags boasting the logos of trendy boutiques jostled each other with friendly grins. Everyone still seemed to be maintaining a holiday mood and goodwill to their fellow man. The "walk" signal flashed abruptly and I nudged my silent companion into motion once more. A workman in a denim coverall and knitted cap was deftly manipulating a screwdriver as he took down a pine wreath from a street light.

Glancing down from his perch in the bucket of the endloader, he nodded a greeting. I smiled back and nimbly skirted a toddler bundled in a parka and muffler. The sight of the child triggered another traitorous memory. One of Andrew's whimsical smiles as he mentioned his hope to one day raise a large family. "If my wife is agreeable, of course," he had added, with an inquiring lift of shaggy brows in my direction.

I winced away from the remembrance. The image obediently vanished and was replaced by the courthouse looming in stately splendor on the right. Dorothea's lips were pressed together tightly and one hand clawed at my sleeve in supplication.

"I can't go through with this, Allyson." She was trembling visibly, eyes anguished.

I halted, oblivious to the press of people around us. I felt the stab of intense empathy for Dorothea, an empathy which I had refused to acknowledge up until now.

"Answer me truthfully, Dorothea. Do you want this divorce? Yes or no? If you don't want it—fine. We'll have it dismissed. Otherwise, we're going to ahead with this hearing."

"I think I want the divorce—but do I have to be there? I haven't faced my husband since I had the papers served on him."

Her lips quivered, dread lurking behind the uneven layers of make-up.

Unaware until we had stopped moving of the strength and bite of the wind, I shivered and studied the face of my companion, attempting to pierce the veil of exhaustion. Mrs. Chapin seemed oblivious of the cold, despite being inadequately clad in a thin coat.

"Yes or no, Dorothea? I need an answer!" My voice was purposely harsh and demanding, stimulating the dazed woman to respond.

"I'm so confused. I guess it's because…I realize now…he doesn't love me anymore!" The forlorn wail was an echo of many similar voices, keening softly in my memory. I flinched away from the anguished sound, demandingly audible, rising above the steady traffic noises form the street.

Dorothea had managed to touch a raw nerve, to spotlight the stumbling block which loomed between Andrew and me. How many times had I heard it? The miserable recital of love, which had faded, become indifferent or turned to snarling, vengeful, hatred. The tales of hurtful words, the low voiced confessions of affairs or of the discovery of a partner's infidelity. Or perhaps the couple no longer cared, merely co-existed in the same house as distantly polite roommates. Neither spouse was able to shatter the cycle of pain unaided. The agonizing emotion of the process and the despairing interviews were beginning to affect my own relationships, my own responses.

I became aware that Dorothea Chapin was regarding me in surprise, startled out of self-absorption by the flicker of distress which must be visible on my face.

Case in Point

"Is something wrong?" she whispered uneasily. In our relationship as attorney—client, I had been a strong confidant, the one who shouldered the burden and kept the divorce moving toward fruition. Now it seemed to her that the last bastion of defense had been challenged and found unsteady.

With an effort, I pulled myself together and spoke in a reassuring tone. "I'm ready to proceed. Are you?"

"Let's get it over with—the suspense of waiting is making me ill." Her voice broke on the last words.

The divorce court was located on the fourth floor of the building which housed our county judicial system. I led the way out of the elevator onto the familiar black and white tiles. The squares reminded me of a narrow chessboard, with the hallway's occupants the chessmen whose steps mirrored their decisions in reality. Moving forward, retreating, changing the balance of power—with personal happiness the prize for victory.

The hall was crowded; divorce court was a very popular place these days. Suddenly I froze, breath catching painfully at the sight of a familiar tilt to one man's head.

Andrew threaded his way with determination through the throng of attorneys and clients with a thin, studious looking man in tow. The sight of Andrew's broad shoulders straining the tweed of his suit sent a quiver of excitement dancing up my spine.

With an abrupt gesture, he grasped my arm above the elbow and drew me away from my startled client, his rugged features in a startling contrast to the gentleness of the spirit existing within the husky frame. Mrs. Chapin remained frozen by the bank of elevators, cringing away from the confused hubbub of many voices.

"Andrew! What are you doing here? I thought we agreed not to see each other for a few days." I kept my voice low, but indignant.

"I was pining away for a glimpse of your brown eyes," he retorted and grinned at the resulting sparks the remark generated. "I'm a gentleman. I keep my word. Bill Douglas went home at 10:00 a.m. with the flu and they dumped the Chapin divorce file on my desk. As an associate attorney, I have to bark when they say 'speak'. Your name was listed as opposing counsel and I thought I'd better prepare you for the shock of seeing me before you had an audience."

I stiffened angrily at his rallying tone but with a quick change of subject, he moved to the case at hand.

"Are you and your client ready to proceed, Allyson? My client informs me that his soon-to-be-ex-wife is, and I quote, 'A watering pot with creeping tendrils winding into his wallet'."

'He didn't say that, did he?' A reluctant smile accompanied my question as I visualized Dorothea leafing out before my eyes.

"Allyson, the man is an English professor! His abuse of the language indicates how much this situation has affected him. Is Mrs. Chapin willing to back down from her stand on the maintenance issue? You must be aware that she not only wants the shirt off his back, but also has an eye on his cuff links and the gold fillings in his teeth."

I withdrew my sleeve from his grasp with dignity. "No comment. We've made our position quite clear in our correspondence with your firm. See you in court, Mr. Stevenson."

Returning to the little eddy in the current of traffic which indicated where I had abandoned my client, I gritted my teeth. He could he speak to me in such a teasing manner after our bittersweet parting? Didn't he understand the turmoil and emotional upheaval I was going through?

Pausing outside the courtroom, I discovered that our case was third in line on the call-up sheet. We entered the echoing room with its cold marble floor and hard chairs. Following an ancient tradition, we, as plaintiffs, chose the right-hand side of the room while the defendants seated themselves on the left.

During the wait to appear, I reflected back over my relationship with the man sitting across the room. Introduced at a Bar Association meeting through the happy accident of his spilling coffee on my skirt (to this day he refused to admit that it had been on purpose), our warm friendship gradually began to change into something deeper, more personal.

Our date Sunday evening had been spent viewing some of the Christmas lighting displays that were still in place. Over the last two weeks, Andrew had been attempting to intrude plans for the future into the relationship while I struggled to hold him at arm's length. The intoxication of Andrew's presence, however, was beginning to bulldoze through my defenses. A kiss could make me dangerously agreeable.

Case in Point

At the bailiff's direction, the assembled gathering rose with a rustling of coats and files to honor the entrance of the judge. I followed suit automatically, my mind still on our last meeting.

Parked on a hill overlooking the city, with the twinkling lights below and the stars gleaming above, Andrew had conjured up a thermos of hot chocolate from under the front seat of his car. We toasted each other with steaming mugs before we kissed deeply, delightfully. Andrew then displayed the ring as it nestled on a bed of velvet, refracting the light of a thousand stars, his declaration of love falling on my ears with the sweet ring of truth. I felt a deep surge of love in return for this bear-sized man and had actually parted my lips to speak—to accept the proposal offered so beautifully.

Suddenly harsh echoes of the past few weeks clambered in my head, the tears, the vanished love, the broken marriages. Wincing away from the ring cradled in his hands, I had pleaded for time. Time to consider, time to gain the courage to reject or accept him.

The first case was going forward swiftly; it was a "civilized" divorce. Mrs. Chapin was following the proceedings with breathless interest, lips parted; her mask of tense withdrawal had been stripped away. I glanced over at Andrew. His head was bent over some papers removed from his briefcase, reassuring his client with his tranquil confidence.

Could I refuse when a man offered me his heart? Did I love him enough to take a gamble on marriage? I wanted someone to assure me that divorce wouldn't rear its ugly head to shatter my happiness. I'd seen it happen often to my friends; the very thought was devastating. Other brides had taken this important step with confidence shining in their eyes. Why did I hesitate?

The next case was called. The couple glared at each other around their respective counsel, bitter lines evident around the husband's mouth. I shuddered. Would the flame of love and passion turn into ashes for me as well?

Images from the past rose up to offer evidence in Andrew's favor. There was the night spent at the hospital while my mother underwent emergency surgery. Desperately afraid and alone, I dialed his number with shaking hands. When he answered in a haze of sleep, I blurted out my fears in a torrent of words. Ignoring the time factor of 2:00 a.m., he had responded by padding into the lobby within minutes, pajamas concealed under a trench coat and eased the endless hours of waiting with a strong arm around my shoulders. Throughout the long, agonizing minutes, the impression of drafty corridors and starched, rustling staff workers was overshadowed by the warmth and power of his hand in mine.

Another slide clicked into the viewer of memory. Early last spring, I had been stricken with a mild case of bronchitis. Unable to gather the strength to fix a meal, wash dishes or pour a glass of orange juice, I huddled in bed and wondered with despair who I could call for assistance. The impersonal, modern apartment building in which I lived had not yielded any close friends among my neighbors.

Interrupted in a bout of self-pity by a knock on the door, I staggered out to find Andrew on my doorstep clutching a bag of oranges and grapefruit, a plush pink teddy bear in tribute to my nickname for him, and a bouquet of glorious daffodils. Bursting into tears of relief, he tucked me back into bed and dosed me with fresh citrus fruit and penicillin. Andrew then straightened up the apartment and washed a load of sheets and towels. Undeterred by my cough, red nose and streaming eyes, he had remained to sit by the bed and offer comfort and companionship.

My turn to repay his kindness had come when his father was stricken with a fatal heart attack. I drove Andrew to the airport on a Sunday evening, listening quietly to his rambling discourse on his relationship with his father and the agonized self-examination as to why he hadn't been there when it happened. Just before boarding the plane, Andrew turned back and enfolded me in a close embrace, squeezing my breath out with the strength of his feelings.

I could never forget the good times: picnics, rides in the country, sitting by the fire watching the light play on his reddish hair, exploring our differing views and opinions with a passion. We had sipped together from the mixture of the joy and pain which made up the potion of love, both ingredients inexorably intertwined. We had a powerful bond between us—one that was mysterious, priceless, timeless. Why then was I still afraid?

Case in Point

"Case of Chapin v. Chapin," the clarion voice of the bailiff jerked me back to the present and the cold somberness of the courtroom. I became aware that Mrs. Chapin was gripping the back of the seat in front of them with white knuckled hands. Mr. Chapin and Andrew emerged from the crowd with deliberation and took their places at the neighboring counsel table, Mr. Chapin regarding his wife with sad resignation.

The judge rubbed the bridge of his nose wearily before replacing his glasses and picking up the court file.

"Is counsel ready?" He glanced wistfully at the clock in the rear of the courtroom as he spoke, hoping that it was time to adjourn.

As attorney for the petitioner, it was up to me to start the proceedings. Before I could speak, however, a sob burst from Dorothea Chapin, the pent-up emotions breaking through.

"No! I've changed my mind! I don't want a divorce!"

The murmur of conversation from the spectators and attorneys present in the courtroom stilled as the echoes of a woman's passionate declaration hung quivering in the air.

Andrew and I remained frozen in disbelief, my weakening knees forcing me to grip the edge of the counsel table for support. Mr. Chapin dodged around the massive form of his attorney and hurried to his spouse, words tumbling out in a rush of excitement.

"Do you mean it, Dorothea? If you'll come back to me, I promise I'll try to give you the happiness you deserve. I love you! If you want to take classes at the University, get a job, do more entertaining or travel, it's all right with me. I'm lost without you, darling—I can't find a matched pair of socks or figure how to work the dishwasher. I'm so lonely, Dorothea. I want our marriage to stay intact!"

"I do love you, darling, but you've been so cold and indifferent lately. I don't want expensive presents—I want you! You've been working these extra hours and I didn't feel like I was important any more…"

A man of action, Mr. Chapin cut this tearful disclosure short by seizing his wife and pulling her against his chest in a might embrace.

The judge raised silver brows, bemused by the tender scene being enacted before the bench. The wooden countenance of the bailiff, however, never changed expression as he inquired as to whether I wished to dismiss the case?

Half an hour later, the newly reunited Mr. and Mrs. Chapin departed the scene without a backwards glance or a word of farewell. Andrew and I took our refuge in a deserted conference room to close the file.

"Bill will never assign another case to me again," Andrew chuckled, loosening his tie. "We lost our fee for the court appearance and I just stood there with my jaw hanging down to my chest!"

"I hope they follow up with some type of professional counselling," I murmured. Andrew's presence seemed to fill the tiny room, confusing me with his nearness. I babbled on. "I could tell she was reconsidering. Sometimes the process moves along so fast that the client is unable to think, unable to realize what they have committed themselves to do."

Andrew dropped the slim case folder of the Chapins' marital discord on the table and moved a step closer. I was trembling inside. The shadow of the unanswered proposal hovered between us as the only barrier.

My thoughts in a turmoil, I backed away. I felt compelled to speak—to slice through the glossy façade of the professional relationship to which we still clung.

"Let's forget about the Chapins. I want to talk about us."

Andrew's eyes were dark with suppressed emotion; I could sense that he was reaching out to me but I still fought for freedom.

"I'm not ready to give you an answer yet. I need more time!"

Andrew tried to speak, but I stopped him with a light touch on his lips. "I'm not sure if I'm ready for such a change in our relationship. I don't want what happened to the Chapins to tear us apart! I've seen it happen. I couldn't bear the agony of losing you, my teddy bear." I tried to laugh at the involuntary pun but tears filled my eyes.

With compassion, he placed gentle hands on my shoulders. I bit back a sob of indecision at the warmth generated by his touch and gazed despairingly at one of the buttons on his suit coat. If only he'd get angry, roar, break the tension somehow. Why didn't he say something?

A firm hand lifted my chin to meet his eyes and he spoke quietly and sincerely. "Allyson, honey, listen to yourself. You want us to draw up a formal contract, a guarantee that our marriage won't fail. Love doesn't bring a guarantee. It brings a commitment. When I repeat the words "for richer, for poorer, in sickness and in health, until death do us

Case in Point

part", it will be a vow. You have to accept my word. That's where the trust comes into being. Love and trust are the only basis for a good, lasting marriage. There must be a commitment between two people. I can't make the commitment on your behalf, sweetheart. I can only offer you mine."

The last brick in the barrier I had built to protect myself from pain crumbled at his words. My course seemed blindingly clear; it was as though the sun had suddenly broken through dark clouds with radiant light.

"I love you, Teddy Bear. I will accept your love, your trust and I give you my heart in return," I whispered.

He took me in his arms and I raised my face for his kiss. The verdict was in; both parties were satisfied with the result.

Another attorney flung open the door and we exploded into helpless laughter, clinging to one another, and overheard this comment as he slammed it shut.

"We'll have to find an empty room," he grumbled to an unseen client. "There's another reconciliation going on in there. People forget that this is supposed to be a divorce court!"

THE END

Honey, Do You Love Me?

"Don't let Sandi run amuck." Rachel brushed with a weary hand at a curl which promptly sprang back across her left eye.

My niece giggled, alert to the sound of an unfamiliar word, perhaps picturing mud pies and splashy puddles, and skipped down the walkway to the car.

"I'll keep her on a tight leash," I promised my sister.

Rachel nodded, patting her swollen stomach in the absent-minded manner of a woman coming to the end of her term, surprised afresh by her girth and yet, at the same time, reassured that the baby still moved within its dark, private place.

I could bear to watch no longer. "Stay off your feet while we're gone. Rest, woman! That's the whole point of this expedition."

Tugging on the handle of the passenger door, Sandi's dancing feet embodied the impatience of four years young with the tardiness of her elders. "Come on, Aunt Claire!"

My sister grasped my arm. "You all right? Not still brooding about—"

"I'm simply wondering what I'm going to feed the munchkin for lunch. That's all that's on my mind." I forced a bright smile which wouldn't have fooled Sandi and freed myself. "Got to run before she yanks the door off my car."

Once we were on our way, Sandi chatted unself-consciously, her shrill, piping voice competing with the sounds of Saturday morning traffic until she discovered the radio scan button.

Honey, Do You Love Me?

Vintage Motown, rock, rap, and country western, spurted out of the speakers until I switched off the radio. Realized that I preferred the discordant blare over treacle-thick silence.

Bored, my niece appropriated the sunglasses I'd placed on the dash after the sun disappeared behind a cloud.

Perching them on her snub nose, she demanded, "How do I look?"

Her pert tone and confidently uptilted chin proclaimed a conviction that she had been transformed into someone stunning and grown-up. The dark lenses dominated her features, concealing childishly rounded cheeks and huge brown eyes. Strangers frequently mistook Sandi for my own daughter on our frequent outings together. "How sweet! She has your eyes!"

Not today. Mine were red and swollen from crying; the glasses Sandi modeled had been useful earlier in disguising the puffiness when facing my sister.

"You look glamorous. Tres chic, mademoiselle!"

Sandi beamed and the glasses slipped off her nose and tumbled into her lap. I forced an answering smile, my shield of cheerful composure holed by pinpricks of pain.

But the release of tears must be denied until I was once more alone in my apartment, that cavern of loneliness haunted by angry voices and the ghost of a woman sobbing over a stained tablecloth and guttered candles. Party favors from an intimate supper turned into a dreadful parting repast.

"Stop wallowing in self-pity", I chastised myself in disgust. "You'll never be able to climb out of the mire if you continue to dwell on those memories…"

But Ken's clipped voice overrode Sandi's chirping song. "You're an adult, Claire. I thought you always took precautions."

Precautions? Instantly, I was back in the dining room chair facing Ken, the meal prepared with such tender anticipation churning in my stomach. My lover had chosen to accuse me of carelessness, his reaction peevish, as though I'd forgotten the mosquito repellant on a camping trip.

Candle flames cast unfriendly shadows across the cheekbones which my fingertips ached to caress. The food set on the neutral zone of the table which separated us had been prepared with love and nervous expectation. I'd left work three hours early to bake Ken's favorite cherry dessert.

Reflected flames glowed in the eyes which locked onto mine like a target sight. I wondered briefly why I'd always regarded candlelight as romantic.

When Ken spoke again, his tone shifted to relief. "At least this isn't a big deal."

At my sharp, indrawn breath, he frowned in quick rebuke. "Unless you're foolish enough to think about keeping it."

I stiffened in involuntary protest of the pronoun. It? His casual tone might refer to a pencil rolled under the table or a quarter discovered on the sidewalk. Not our child. He was dismissing something forged on the white hot anvil of our love without a second thought.

"I didn't want to consider adoption until we'd had a chance to talk about this—"

"Get rid of it. Now." Ken's voice was flat as the champagne in my glass.

I'd bought the champagne for a celebration, our celebration. My dinner companion raised his glass of wine and took a noisy sip, the omission of a toast deliberate and cruel. To us?

My mouth dried as the strong fingers which knew my pleasure zones so intimately gripped his glass in a stranglehold, betraying the tension he refused to allow into his voice.

I swallowed the lump formed from unshed tears. "What if I don't?"

The slender stem of the glass snapped like a fragile bone and I recoiled from the sound. Ken moved his hand in an angry arc and the wine bottle he'd insisted on uncorking before dinner tipped over and passion red, blood red liquid flowed across my best linen tablecloth.

His temper escaped, mimicking the wine's eager flight, spread out to engulf me. "We can't put our lives on hold, Claire. Not when our relationship is based on freedom, the enjoyment of our sexuality—living life to the fullest! I refuse to be trapped into pushing a designer stroller around the mall."

The bitter set of his mouth betrayed that this last hurtful thrust was intentional. We'd met at a shopping mall nearly six months earlier, exchanging names over fat, salty pretzels. He carried a shopping bag full of black socks with the aplomb of a diamond courier.

"I'm a fanatic about the quality of my socks." Ken's tongue flicked out to lick the salt from the dough's yielding surface. "And my women."

His smile was heart-stopping, darting into the inner core of my being and expanding until it left a void only his love-making could fill.

That smile was nowhere in evidence now and I resented his scornful reference to the site of our first meeting, a place that until tonight I still thought of as magical.

"This is our baby we're discussing, not a bad spot in an apple to be dug out and thrown away!"

The candles sputtered in derisive response to my passion. Drops of wax burned like hot tears on the back of the hand I extended across the table to Ken.

"Touch me, darling," I pleaded. "Hold me close again, tell me you love me. Tell me that everything will be all right."

Instead, he pulled away, as if I'd jabbed him with my fork. "I can't make love to a woman with a belly like a sack of potatoes. I don't want a brat whining for attention. Make your choice, Claire. You can have the baby—or you can have me."

* * * *

Once in the department store, Sandi had a difficult time choosing a toy. The visual testimony of my dilemma concealed again behind the dark glasses, I watched my niece sort through a selection of plastic balls.

"This one," she said suddenly with the conviction of a mother hen picking out her chick form the scattered flock.

Her choice featured a design of floppy-eared puppies in a basket. As I made the proper appreciative comments, a woman pushing a stroller—a designer stroller—down the narrow aisle begged our pardon. We moved aside.

I caught myself patting the waistband of my shorts in an unconscious imitation of Rachel's gesture and jerked my hand away as though the material had been threaded with red hot wires.

A nearby sign decorated with a tumbling clown pointed the way to the maternity clothes. A child hurried past bearing a golden-haired baby doll in her arms. To me, the air seemed suffocatingly thick. Cloying whiffs from the perfume counter mingled with the fresh, clean scent of the powder patted onto Sandi's soft skin after her morning bath.

I couldn't help my runaway thoughts. Yesterday, drained from hours of weeping, I had curled up in the closet which still contained an elusive hint of Ken's cologne and reached a decision.

I wanted this baby. But without Ken, I would shrivel up like a plant denied the life-giving rays of the sun. He had been gone for less than two weeks and I already hated eating alone every night, dreaded facing the lonely expanse of the bed.

My lover's ultimatum could be read in the jangling, hanger-filled emptiness of the closet, in his absence in the bed where we'd made what I thought was love every night.

I could see it in the absence of his shaving cream in the cabinet, and in three scribbled sentences on a note stuck to the refrigerator with a Huckleberry Hound magnet. "I want you, Claire. Just you. Call me if you want me."

"I want you, Ken," I whispered.

A tug on my hand brought me back to the present; I winced from the renewed assault of the kaleidoscopic displays and piped-in music on my strained nervous system.

"Let's go to the park and play with my new ball," Sandi suggested.

I'd promised to keep custody of my niece until at least five o'clock. Sandi, displaying the budding of exotic tastes, chose rum raisin from the flavor selection available in the frosted depths of the ice cream wagon parked in the shade of an ancient oak. After a few tentative licks, however, she proposed an exchange and I handed over my sensible strawberry cone.

The morning clouds had vanished and the sun beat down on my uncovered head. Black ants and lady bugs accepted the barrier of my sandal-clad feet as a detour through the grass. My legs were still slim, but I punished myself by picturing them puffy and blue-veined in the last stage of pregnancy.

Honey, Do You Love Me?

Sand pranced up. After twenty minutes of energetic motion, the exposed flesh around the neckline of her sunsuit had turned bright pink and beads of perspiration darkened her hairline.

"Come sit with me," I coaxed, moving into the shade.

She reluctantly collapsed onto the blanket I'd unearthed from the clutter of belongings in the trunk of my car and cradled the ball in her lap. Leaning against my shoulder, she began her favorite game, head tilted back to catch the first glimmer of a smile on my face.

"Honey, do you love me?"

The proper response came easily to my lips. "Honey, I love you, but I just can't smile."

She seemed pleased. Her small, quivering body generated the radiant heat of a furnace and I reached down to mop up the clear drops of perspiration that glimmered like crystal tears on her upturned face.

"Honey, do you love me?"

"Honey, I love you, but I just can't smile."

Again, "Honey, do you love me?", this time injecting wistfulness into her tone while wrinkling her nose comically, a sun-pinked bunny sniffing a succulent lettuce leaf.

Her gaze was fixed on my mouth, her eyes alert for the smile that was the signal of victory and her cue to pounce for a free-for-all tickling assault.

"Honey, I love you—"

The remainder of the ritualistic reply stuck in my throat. I'd screamed the first part, those very words, at Ken's back and had been answered by a door slam.

The sunglasses fell to the ground as I covered my face and wept, only dimly aware of Sandi's hands clutching my elbow in distress.

"Aunt Claire, don't cry! Don't cry! We don't have to play!"

I tried to look at her through burning, streaming eyes. Instead of her piquant features, however, I saw the eyes of my unborn babe staring imploringly back at me.

Ken or the unseen child? Choosing the baby meant being forever denied Ken's caress, never again sipping coffee together while bathed in morning sunshine with the Sunday papers scattered across a bed rumpled from making love. Doing without Ken meant raising a child alone and pushing that designer stroller on solitary walks.

My heart was a stone, calcified in the moment of betrayal, of coming home to find no evidence that the man had ever inhabited my life except for the faint scent of cologne and his seed growing within me...

Sandi patted my shoulder with tender concern. "Aunt Claire, did you hurted yourself?"

I had loved and lost. I'd offered up my vulnerable soul for repudiation. I wiped at the tears with a corner of the blanket. "Yes, darling, I did."

"When I fell down yesterday, Mommy kissed my sore knee and made it better."

We stared at each other, aunt and niece. Supplicant and wise woman. The wind rustled the leaves of nearby trees, providing faint applause to the solemn, dramatic climax of the scene.

"Some hurts are too deep for kisses, Sandi," I managed at last. "But a loving kiss always helps."

She scrambled to her knees and kissed my damp cheek with a zestful smack. Giggled. "You taste salty, like a pretzel."

Greek tragedy followed by a stand-up comic routine. The ending of a relationship begun over a pretzel had been sealed by a pretzel kiss. My lips shaped a feeble grin at the irony.

"You smiled! I win!"

Sandi tossed her ball into the air, sparking a wild game of soccer in which three other children and a cocker spaniel joined in. Watching the exuberant participants with envy, I longed for the ability to enter Sandi's protected world, where a smile meant security and kisses healed all wounds.

If I closed my eyes, I could imagine Ken's arms around me. But he couldn't—wouldn't—make love to a woman with a belly like a sack of potatoes.

A robin stalked past on fragile legs. I reflected on how the males of the animal world often deserted their mates during gestation. Honoring no commitment, they choose instead to live without responsibility while the female raises the young alone, defends her offspring with tooth and claw.

Honey, Do You Love Me?

Although I still ached to feel Ken's fingers entwined in my hair and nibble his skin again, the memory of that slammed door echoed in my head.

What if instead of pregnancy temporarily reshaping my body, an accident permanently scarred my face? Or my breasts—which Ken called "my beauties" and fondled like precious gems—were invaded by cancer cells? Would he pack his bags for departure while I lay helpless in a hospital bed?

A tune ran through my head, a ditty chanted when I was a child. Looking back, that singer had been breathtaking in her naiveté. Love and marriage don't always go together like a horse and carriage. Without commitment, infatuation burns at passion's white hot, fever pitch but when the inevitable cooling takes place, nothing lasting has been forged. Only ashes remain, dead, gray ashes.

I had never played Sandi's game with Ken. Honey, do you love me? Yes, honey, I love you, but only on my terms...

The taste of ashes filled my mouth. Bitter, charred, dead. My relationship with Ken had existed only on a mundane physical plane; the spiritual heights of ecstasy had been attained only in my imagination.

Sandi squealed. The ball skimmed across the grass, leaving no permanent track or evidence of its passage.

"Let's go home and help your mom fix dinner."

On the way back to the car, I carried the blanket and Sandi clutched the carryall. She walked sedately by my side, the reclaimed, oversized sunglasses sliding down her nose, giving my little waif the jaunty air of a child starlet on an outing with her nanny.

A bed of tulips caught her hopscotch attention and she rushed over to examine the blossoms just beginning to unfold, their furled petals concealing the mystery of color.

"Can I pick one of these for Mommy?" Sandy asked, a chubby finger stroking a tightly curled bud.

I crouched, too, the breeze ruffling my hair, and faced the knowledge that the hollowness within me came not from Ken's rejection, but from my futile desire to reclaim that which was irrevocably lost.

Ken made his decision. I must make mine.

My heart gave a funny little leap, like a lamb in springtime, and I kissed my niece's flushed cheek. "The flower will bloom and become beautiful for everyone to enjoy if you let it grow, Sandi. Such things only get better with time."

Behind us, the robin rose into the air with the promise of new life in the beat of its wings.

THE END

The Friendship Ring

Except for a new jungle gym and the fresh coating of paint on the picnic tables, the park hadn't changed, April thought. Switching off the ignition, she turned to her daughters. "Would you like to stretch your legs before we go to the apartment and unpack the car?"

Filled with pent-up energy after hours of travel, they shouted a gleeful assent. The chubby legs of three year old Beth churned across the grass as she headed for the kiddie swings, April following more slowly. Annie, conscious of the dignity of an added four years, walked over to watch other children on the seesaws.

After making sure the safety belt was fastened across Beth's tummy, April gave the swing a gentle push. Beth shrieked with delight, but April barely heard her, her mind drifting back to a spring evening thirteen years ago. Despite what she had told the girls, this stop was more for their mother's benefit: April was here to exorcise two ghosts, one of whom was her younger self.

Although her curfew was midnight, she and Kevin had paused here on the walk home from the senior high dance to exchange playful kisses in the shadows of the ancient oak trees.

The equipment and grassy expanse had been deserted; all of the children who earlier had swung and played tag were tucked into bed. Kevin took April's hand, drew her away from the watchful eye of the street light, and kissed her again, tenderly at first, the demands of his mouth quickly becoming more urgent.

April kissed him back, the music still lilting in her heart.

Suddenly, Kevin's mouth no longer covered hers; his hands gripped her arms. "I love you, April."

Caught up in the spell of diamond bright stars sparkling through the leafy branches arching overhead, April stared up at him, bewildered. "Love?"

His fingers touched her lips in a hushing gesture. "I have no right to speak now—to selfishly try to hold you—but you must know I want to spend the rest of my life with you."

"Oh, no!" April breathed the words in dismay; the iridescent bubble of college plans and freedom which hovered on the horizon like the bright new moon burst with an almost audible "pop" in the tranquility of the night.

Kevin's fervent declaration frightened her. His future was already mapped out: a local college, law school, and then back home to take over his father's practice.

She tried to erase his words. "It's too soon to talk of love, Kevin. I'm going away next month and between holding down a part-time job and studying, I probably won't be able to come home on weekends. When would we see each other?"

"If we love each other, April, we can find ways to keep our relationship alive. Whenever I think of doing without the sound of your laughter, that saucy toss of your head when someone teases you—even the earnest way you lick an ice cream cone, my heart aches and I don't want to face the future."

She retreated into the moonlight away from the fervor in his tone, her slippers sliding on the dew dampened grass. "Kevin, you're confusing me. I'm not ready for a commitment!"

"I can't keep silent any longer." He raked his fingers through his hair. "It's too close to a separation I'm afraid will be final. When I gave you that friendship ring at Christmas, I was a coward for not admitting the ring was really a token of my love."

April looked down at her hand. The narrow gold ribbon weighed down her finger like an iron band, holding her earthbound when she wanted to soar, fettering her to a life of predictability with a man she

The Friendship Ring

knew too well. Kevin was already tied down with responsibility, a hostage to his father's expectations.

Panicked, she wrenched the ring from her finger and flung it away as if the metal burned her flesh, the ring's glittering arc immediately swallowed up by the grass and shadows…

"Push me, Mama! Push!" Beth's imperious demands brought April back from the past and into the fading summer sunshine.

Dropping a kiss on the child's curls, April set the swing into motion again. "Just a few more minutes."

Beth wriggled in the seat, warbling a tuneless, baby song, and April glanced over at Annie. Her daughter was clambering up the jungle gym and chattering to another girl. If Annie was dropped by parachute into a foreign country in the morning, she'd have a network of friends established by dusk, April reflected, grateful for the child's bubbly personality which would ease the transition into a new school.

A familiar baritone jolted her. "What'll it be, Joseph? Swings, sandbox, or slide?"

April whirled, Beth's happy chant fading in her ears. Kevin stood a few feet away, one hand clutching the fingers of a toddler with enormous blue eyes.

Kevin. Kevin and a son who had eyes so like his father's that April's heart somersaulted in her chest. *Why are you surprised?* A voice in her head mocked her. In a town this size, it was only natural that Kevin would bring his child to the park where he himself had played.

"April!" Kevin rushed forward. Crushed against his chest in a hug of genuine warmth that brought tears to her eyes, she heard him exclaim, "Let me look at you!"

He held her at arm's length. "Hair's still honey blonde and no man could forget those knockout eyes the rich brown of molasses. A fine wine couldn't have aged better."

April bit her lip, tasted blood before responding. "The combination of honey and molasses sounds revoltingly sweet. How are you, Kevin?"

He continued, ignoring the question. "Almost couldn't believe my ears when a school board member mentioned you'd applied for a teaching position. I thought when you shook the dust of our town from your sandals that we'd never see you again, especially after your parents moved to Florida."

She listened for a sting behind the words, but heard only ordinary politeness and matched his tone. "I've just arrived and the girls are burning off surplus energy before we unpack the car. I guess it's no coincidence running into you here."

Kevin grinned. "Weather permitting, as soon as I get home I put on my jeans and we hike over for a little fun together."

"He's adorable." April studied the boy crouched beside the sandbox and now engaged in pouring sand into a tiny pail. Resentment swelled in her breast towards Joseph's mother, the woman perceptive enough to accept Kevin as the wonderful husband and father he undoubtedly was. I was too young to know what I wanted, she thought.

"Is this your little sweetheart?" Kevin knelt to make Beth's acquaintance and April decided that a business suit couldn't look any better on his long legged form than the snug blue jeans.

"That's Beth." The little girl giggled when he patted her knee.

"How long have you been married? Any other kids?"

"Annie's over there, she's seven." April pointed towards the jungle gym. "I'm not married anymore."

The simple sentence couldn't begin to cover the heartbreak resulting from her husband's announcement that he was seeking a divorce because he'd fallen in love with his receptionist. Rob's new bride didn't want children—at least not Annie and Beth.

So far, Beth seemed for the most part unaware of her father's desertion, but gallant Annie's sufferings surfaced in nightmares and midnight bouts of tears. Desperate to provide the security her daughters needed, the only solution which came to April's mind was a move back to where she had flourished in an atmosphere of love.

Seeking to brush over the awkward pause, April smiled at Joseph. "Is he your first?"

"And only." Kevin's mouth tightened before he continued, "His mother died about a year ago in a car accident."

As he spoke, April saw the flash of pain in his eyes. She felt guilty and confused—embarrassed at having envied a dead woman. Knowing

The Friendship Ring

that Kevin was free again added to the tension and she turned to help Beth out of the swing, avoiding his gaze.

Did he think she had come looking for him because her marriage failed? Face burning, she perceived that applying for a job here had been the act of a child seeking to alter the past. Her vehement rejection of Kevin's love had haunted her, perhaps even contributed to the failure of her own marriage. Subconsciously, she might have unfairly compared Rob to Kevin, seeing in her husband only a shadow of the qualities which made this man so special.

April realized she was staring at the stand of oaks where her younger self had faced a crossroads and taken the wrong turning. Seeking love and fulfillment out in the world, when she'd already held the precious treasure in her hand and chose to throw it away. I didn't know, she reflected sorrowfully, but my immaturity was no excuse for behaving with such cruelty.

"You probably won't feel up to making supper tonight and I've got a roast in the slow cooker that's too big for the two of us." Kevin dusted the sand from the knees of his small son's overalls. "How about coming over for a hot meal?"

A dark lock of hair curled against his forehead. April remembered the feel of it, silky smooth, and suddenly she couldn't bear the kindness in his voice. Time's river had flowed between them, carving a chasm too deep to cross. They must part as strangers, but she had something to say first.

April gripped Beth's hand tightly for courage. "Remember what happened the last time we were in this park?"

A sigh, wistful as the wind in trees. "I remember."

"All these years I've wanted to tell you…" Her throat closed up with tears and she swallowed hard. "To tell you that I'm sorry."

He was silent, granting her the dignity to continue. "I couldn't sleep knowing that I'd hurt you. At 5:30 the next morning, I was back here crawling on my knees in the wet grass looking for the ring. Not finding it, I lacked the courage to apologize and when I think of what might have been—"

"You know, 'might have been' are three of the saddest words in the English language." Kevin stooped and picked up a small object lying on the ground near a picnic table. "But they're only words. Powerless words. This isn't gold, but maybe it will do. Hold out your hand."

She watched as Kevin slipped a cigar band on her finger. "Once love is given, it can't be lost in the grass, April, or thrown away, but becomes a part of your soul and enriches your life forever."

His eyes seemed to look back over the vanished years and dismiss them. "Consider this a token of friendship. Now the lost ring is no longer a barrier between us."

Her gaze dropped to the narrow paper circle. It was light, insubstantial as thistledown on her finger, but she cherished it as a symbol of hope, of new beginnings, more than any golden band. The past was the pat, but with the warmth of his gaze, Kevin was telling her that the wonderful future awaited her—perhaps them.

Beckoning to Annie, April smiled back at Kevin. "I accept your offer of a hot meal. And friendship."

THE END

Sleeping with Dr. Dee

My personal train of disaster left the station the day Petey borrowed his sister's toy mop to scrub the bathroom floor. While disagreeing with his method of execution, I appreciated his logic. To a two year old, bothering with a bucket is ridiculous when one has a handy source of water in the toilet.

While he was thus engaged, I dozed, oblivious, with my cheek pillowed on the bills I was supposed to be paying. I'd been up all night with Emily who suffered from both a bad cold and a particularly nasty nightmare. While the children were napping snug in their beds, I mistakenly allowed my own heavy lids to close.

I awoke only when the splashing in the toilet reached the crescendo of a shark feeding frenzy. Not content with flooding the bathroom, Petey had enlisted the aid of his older brother and sister in cleaning the hallway carpeting.

When my husband arrived home, expecting the scents and sight of a sustaining meal, he found his wife clearing the dining room of toys and three children still sulking that their attempt to help Mommy had been so cruelly spurned.

Sighing like a man who's just learned that the football game has been pre-empted by a televised presidential speech, Alan loosed his tie and pitched in to help. I stiffened at the implied rebuke in that sigh. My day had been as equally exhausting as his and not nearly as well compensated.

"It's been a long day," I muttered. "The children tried to help me."

"Ah." Alan didn't say it like someone about to pour the balm of understanding on a wounded spirit. It was more of I'm-tired-of-coming-home-to-a-mess-again type of "ah", the kind that always sets my lips in a firm line.

After the birth of our youngest, I'd deserted the hectic world of part-time real estate sales for the even more chaotic one of full-time parenting. Days like today made the problem of selling a luxury townhouse situated near an incinerator sound like a pleasant challenge.

Blessing casseroles that come in a box, I whipped dinner into the oven and then onto the table, which Alan had set. Conversation lagged over the uninspired meal like a kid with a pebble in his shoe; the children were sullen and feeling unappreciated and, frankly, so was I.

After the usual struggle, the trio of trouble was bathed, read to, and tucked into bed. Alan and I were stacking dishes in the dishwasher when he finally mumbled, "Tough day, huh?"

"You have no idea," I said, rinsing the casserole dish. Hoping to prolong our little tete-a-tete, I decided to share an amusing incident that had happened today in the grocery store.

Before I could plunge into my story, however, Alan wiped his hands on a dishtowel and kissed the air in the vicinity of my cheek. "Pre-game starts in ten minutes. Gonna warm up the set."

I'd rather he warmed up his wife. Slam-dunking a glass, I realized that the bloom was definitely off the marital rose. Alan's a wonderful father and, when he can be induced to concentrate on me instead of a job, crabgrass, or televised sports, a thoughtful husband and lover. Musing on the urgency of adding spice to our stew of wedded bliss, I crammed the casserole dish into a space only big enough for a cup, added soap, and switched on the dishwasher.

I was wiping down the countertops and trying to come up with a plan to shorten the pro basketball season, when the phone rang.

Estelle's familiar trill. "Rose, you bad girl! Fancy keeping it a secret! You are too smart for words!"

I made my usual witty response when accused of cleverness. "Huh?"

"Winnie called me. Peg called Winnie. Nancy called Peg—by now it's probably all over town."

Sleeping with Dr. Dee

I still was groping in the dark. "It? Estelle, what are you babbling about?"

"He's so intense! A little short and on the chunky side, but I like a man to be solid. He seems so understanding—most mothers swear by his bedside manner." A girlish giggle. "And those hands! Strong and slim, made to explore a woman's most secret places. But then, I don't have to tell you about that."

Her sly emphasis, as well as her words, had me completely baffled. Was she describing a romance hero or a gynecologist?

When she paused for breath, I snatched the conversational reins away from her. "Estelle, would you kindly stop blathering and tell me who and what you're talking about?"

Silence. Then, in a hurt voice, she said, "I thought we were friends, Rose. Don't friends share things? Okay, keep the juicy details to yourself then. After all, it's your affair."

A click in my ear and I was listening to the dial tone. Deciding that Estelle needed a vacation from monitoring the gossip, I grabbed an apple from the fruit bowl. Before I could sink my teeth into its firm flesh, the meaning of Estelle's coy innuendos sank in.

I snatched up the phone and dialed her number, brushing aside her rather grumpy greeting. "Spill it, Estelle! What rumor has tarred my reputation?"

"It's all over town, Rose. As your friend, I'm disappointed at being one of the last to know. But Nancy was actually there, in the grocery store with you. She heard what Petey said. Out of the mouth of babes…"

"But Nancy misunderstood—"

"Rose, I know how it is. I sympathize, believe me. I just should have put it together sooner. You've been complaining about all the hours Alan's been spending at the office and then in the next breath telling me that you took poor Emily to the doctor again for a sore throat or earache or something."

During this speech, I'd been frantically trying to break in with a refutation, but Estelle rolled on with the momentum of a ten ton boulder. "You should have told me, Rose. I can keep a secret."

Dazed, I cut the connection, remembering the incident. I'd hushed Petey immediately, thinking we were alone near the frozen pizzas, but

Nancy and her ferret-keen ears must have been lurking in an adjoining aisle. Close enough to hear the announcement uttered in a two year old's most piercing tones: "This morning Mommy slept with Dr. Dee!"

Despite Estelle's cutesy remarks about strong hands exploring a woman's secret places, Dr. Dee is a pediatrician, and a good one. He's probably five years younger than I am and wears heavy black glasses, the type Cary Grant used to flaunt in his more scholarly movie roles.

Dr. Dee is married, has tots of his own, and a thriving practice. Which may or may not continue to flourish now that a distorted truth is travelling the town informational super highway. Petey was correct—I did sleep with Dr. Dee this morning.

Since Estelle was out of reach, I bit into the apple. It tasted bitter. The phone chirped and I picked it up with a cautious hand.

"Hi, Rose."

"Karen!" I nearly burst into tears of relief. "I'm glad it's you."

"You won't be after I get through scolding you. We've got to talk, girlfriend."

"Don't talk about friendship—I've already been subjected tonight to Estelle's twisted version. And, Karen, before you condemn, I've got an explanation."

"Did you sleep with Dr. Dee?" my best friend demanded. "I've heard three different versions, including one where the two of you were caught grappling on the kiddie table in the reception area of his office. That account involved building blocks, but the details were just a little bit fuzzy …"

This was a nightmare. "Karen, do you remember a couple of weeks ago when Petey cut his lip on the coffee table?"

"Sure. You hauled him in for stitches and it healed beautifully. Didn't Dr. Dee come in especially to take care of him—Rose, is that when it started?"

"Nothing started! Dr. Dee was kind enough to come to the ER at night since poor Petey absolutely terrified of the doctor on call. He blew up a plastic glove like a balloon and talked in a Donald Duck voice until Petey giggled and only then were we able to get him strapped into the papoose board for the stitches—"

I paused for breath and Karen jumped back in. "Yeah. The doc made

Sleeping with Dr. Dee

quite an impression on Petey on how he took care of his 'mouff' and your son told anyone who would listen."

"Exactly!" I chimed in eagerly. "Petey started calling everyone Dr. Dee, including the dog. Last week he adopted Emily's bald-headed doll and named it Dr. Dee. He slept with that doll, insisted it eat with him, and hauled it around in his red wagon. This morning, I woke up to find the doll tucked under the covers beside me. Emily was sick during the night and Petey beat me getting up—"

I had to quit explaining because of Karen's loud chortling. "I can't believe this," she gasped. "You did sleep with Dr. Dee!"

"Except my Dr. Dee is six inches—not six feet—tall, has no hair, and doesn't snore." I massaged my aching temples. "Not that I know if the real Dr. Dee does. Snore that is. Anyway, Petey was trying to be kind by sharing his doll. He made a general announcement to that effect in the grocery store and Nancy must have overheard him. Stop barking like a hyena, Karen. This could ruin an innocent man's practice, not to mention my reputation!"

Karen stopped gurgling long enough to acknowledge that, yes, I had a problem. The two of us batted various solutions around, but couldn't knock anything over the fence (living with a sports nut has rubbed off on me). When I went in to break the news to Alan that his wife's name was now inextricably linked to another man's, I found him snoring in his chair.

I kissed his bald spot which, to Alan's chagrin, had recently started growing faster than Petey. "Good night, sweet prince. If you don't come to bed soon, I'll call the hospital and see if Dr. Dee's available."

Grunting something unintelligible, my hubby's eyes popped open. "Half time over already? Hon, move over, please. You're in the way and Grant's at the foul line."

Whimpering "Foul!" I retired to a hot bath and some serious thinking. Athletes got compensated for cheap shots—why couldn't wives? Although I was extremely concerned about Dr. Dee's reputation—not to mention my own—I couldn't banish the sneaking suspicion that Alan was taking me for granted.

I discovered over the next several days that squashing a juicy rumor is more difficult than killing the occasional flea that our cocker spaniel picks up in the yard. Rumors can leap higher and quicker than any insect and, like cats, they have more than one life. My attempts at damage control only uncovered several other versions of Dr. Dee and me giving way to our passions in his office, each more titillating than the one involving the blocks and the kiddie table.

Karen checked in occasionally to bray hysterically and report that the wisecracks were running rampant through our strata of friends. After three days of receiving tittering phone calls and cold stares and intercepting knowing glances, I concluded that even Dr. Kevorkian couldn't kill this rumor.

That evening, I caught Alan staring at me over the dish of whipped potatoes I was passing him. "What's the matter? Do I have spinach caught between my teeth?"

He shook his head. "No," he said in a rather strangled murmur. "I was just thinking how lovely you look tonight."

The moment would have been a tad more romantic if the kids hadn't exploded in giggles. Alan continued to gaze at me as though he'd never seen me before. To my surprise, he insisted on helping me clean the kitchen, hovered like an attendant on a suicide watch while I folded laundry, and even kissed the back of my neck as I stood on tiptoe to stack towels in the linen closet.

I turned to confront him. "All right, Alan, what's going on?"

"Going on? I don't know what you mean."

Mr. Innocence in the flesh. Still clutching my armload of towels, I leaned back against the wall. "Isn't there a game tonight? Somewhere in the world some people engaging in some meaningless sport?"

He smiled. A sheepish, guilty grin, just as that kiss had been sheepish and guilty. I'm an excellent lip reader.

Alan chewed the aforementioned object, lower version. "I'd rather spend time with you."

All my inner alarms were going off. "I'd rather you were frank with me. What's going on? Are we broke? Is your Aunt Ada coming for another six week visit? Did you run over Mindy (the cocker spaniel with the occasional flea) in the driveway?"

"No." Alan rubbed his chin. "Honey, we need to talk. I ran into Estelle and her perverted idea of friendship—"

Sleeping with Dr. Dee

Then the other shoe dropped. I widened my eyes in a disingenuous fashion. "And how is dear Estelle?"

"She said some rather disturbing things." Alan's skin had a greenish cast. "Things that made me realize we need to talk."

I put my hand on his arm and said in my most sincere voice, "Alan, what is it? You can tell me. You can trust me to stand behind you, no matter what you've done. Forged checks, committed arson, slept with another woman—"

Alan gulped. He looked like a man who'd just taken a punch below the belt. "Uh, actually, she was talking about, about our marriage being in trouble …"

"Oh, that." I waved an airy hand. "She was probably referring to my affair with Dr. Dee."

Alan was a man stuck in neutral, trying to shift gears while his mental engine raced. "I didn't know—"

"If you count it as an affair." I creased my brow in a pensive frown. "Technically, we only slept together once but I've seen him naked quite a few times."

"Rose! You mean you and the kids' doctor have been—" He groaned, sagging back against the opposite wall. "It's my fault. I haven't been home much and when I'm here I'm usually doing yard work or watching some stupid game on television—"

"True." Grandpa used to tell me that a worm will squirm on the hook as long as you keep his head above water. Although I knew it was wicked, I added, "Petey's really attached to him."

"You've actually been having an affair with Petey's doctor?"

One more squirm to make up for the annual New Year's Day college football marathon. I murmured with downcast eyes, "Dr. Dee listens without interrupting whenever I want to unburden my heart."

Alan raked both hands through his thinning crop of hair. "Rose, tell me the truth. Are you in love with this man?"

Studying my husband's stricken face, I glimpsed the great gulf that yawned between us. Suddenly, the situation didn't seem so funny anymore.

My tongue had somehow turned into a tongue depressor which I manipulated with difficulty. "Alan, if we were truly two souls become one, like we promised each other on our wedding day, we wouldn't be having this conversation."

He said nothing, his lips pressed in a pale line, fear filled eyes searching my face.

I couldn't stop probing the wound. "Alan, we never talk any more. We haven't just drifted apart, we've been swimming in opposite directions."

Still he said nothing. The towels weighing down my left arm had turned to lead, heavy as my heart.

I studied Alan, trying to freeze this moment in my memory. The moment when my safe world crashed down around my head, when I realized that an unseen destroyer had crept in and chewed away the once strong foundations of our marriage.

Alan's slacks and shirt seemed to hang on a body that within the last five minutes had become gaunt. His dear, handsome face was the haggard face of a stranger. Merciful shock held the pain at bay, kept me from falling to the floor and curling into a ball.

He touched my arm. The towels fell in a multi-colored heap at my feet. "Rose, you haven't answered my question."

I watched the warm rain of tears spatter on the backs of my clasped hands. "If you have to ask, Alan—" I choked up.

An eternity passed while we stood there in the narrow passage, inches apart in reality but miles emotionally. The central air sighed on, breathing cool air up through the vent behind me to caress the backs of my legs.

Alan said thickly, "If I have to ask, that means we don't have an ordinary communication gap, but a Grand Canyon between us. I'm ashamed to admit that I don't know you any more, Rose. We've become separate people."

"I'm not having an affair." I spoke quickly, piling words like stones between us. "Petey named that doll he's been lugging around 'Dr. Dee'. He was talking about it in the store the other day, someone misunderstood and started a rumor—"

His hand reached across the yawning gulf, past my makeshift barricade and touched the nape of my neck, as gently as the cool air fanning my legs. "Ever since I talked to Estelle, I've felt as though I've been under a death sentence. Rose, I don't want to live without you. You're a part of me. I know words without action are meaningless, but I love you."

The anguish in his eyes caught at my heart. In a mysterious process, Alan's pain flowed into me, swaddling my bruised spirit and staunching the internal bleeding.

Our faces were a breath apart and we did what we usually did when our lips were in close proximity. But this was no perfunctory kiss, no peck in passing. This was a momentous, earth-shaking exploration, a first-man-on-the-moon venture, a kiss which conducted months of negotiations in an instant and sealed a peace treaty with a gesture more significant than any handshake in history.

We were snuggled together in bed when Alan confessed, "I never would have paid attention to that one woman rumor factory if I didn't already feel so guilty about the way I'd been neglecting you and the kids. For taking you and our marriage for granted, I humbly apologize."

He kissed the tip of my nose and then his lips travelled a penitent path down my throat.

Not fooled by the flowery language, I read sincerity in every caress and allowed his fingers to do the walking on the rest of my body.

Later, I said contentedly, "Estelle's the first to claim friendship, but she has no concept of the real meaning of the word. At least you believe me. Now all I've got to do is come up with a way to save Dr. Dee's marriage."

Alan didn't seem too interested. "Is it in trouble?"

"Wouldn't you feel threatened if you were a woman and you heard that a femme fatale like me was after your husband?"

My lover's hands were making another pilgrimage. "Rose, please say that you forgive me for being an absent husband." He kissed me again.

Since my mouth was otherwise occupied, I knew he didn't really expect me to say anything. I managed, however, to let Alan know that his apology was accepted. Lip reading isn't the only form of communication in which I'm fluent.

The next morning, after Alan had left for the office and the kids were happily splashing in their cereal bowls, I called Karen.

"You've got a definite lilt in your voice," she accused. "Are you sure you aren't having an affair? Only a woman in the throes of new love sounds this happy."

Mindful of listening ears, I lowered my voice. "Alan and I kissed and made up last night."

"If you haven't been involved in a clandestine romance, what exactly were you making up?" Her tone dripped suspicion.

"Lost time." I chirped back. "Listen, Karen, does your friend Joan still write those cutesy feature pieces for the local paper?"

"Yes. But why do—"

"I've decided to go public." I rescued my daughter's cereal bowl, which was in imminent danger of flooding her lap. "I'm going to tell the world about Dr. Dee and me."

Karen called Joan and Joan came through, with a sweet piece about my son's devotion to the doctor who had sacrificed his evening to stitch up a little boy's lip and the form Petey's hero worship took.

The coverage included a photo of Petey with both Dr. Dees and a quote from me: "Petey's been very generous about sharing his doll. We never know which family member will wake up and find it tucked in beside them. We've all slept with Dr. Dee."

Dr. Dee had the article framed and hung in his waiting room. Several of my friends actually apologized to me for believing the worst. Petey soon abandoned both his hero worship and the doll, but "sleeping with Dr. Dee" is now a private code between Alan and me to remind us of what we so nearly lost.

Sitting in Dr. Dee's waiting room recently with Emily, I was paging through a national women's magazine and came across an article wherein a therapist made the controversial claim that a change of bed partners could actually be beneficial to a relationship.

Which brings me to yesterday. Hearing a rumor that Estelle Pendelton's marriage is on the rocks, I went to the library, photocopied that article from the magazine, and mailed it to her. That's what friends are for.

THE END

Half of My Heart

(France; 1949)

The directrice was speaking again, her heavily accented English hammering out the words in explosive syllables.

"We are careful to supervise the studies and the religious background for the children. They study hard, very hard. It is the only way to improve, to advance one's self."

The starkness of the office furnishings were reflected in the wooden chair which bit sharply into the backs of my knees, a crucifix hanging behind the desk the only ornament on the glaring, white walls. France seemed more than an ocean away from Kansas, it was a war-torn world where English was rarely spoken and the triumph of victory had blurred into the reality of a chaotic economy and a list of the dead.

"No one will adopt him because of the mixed parentage. A German mother and a French-Jewish father; c'est impossible!" A despairing gesture emphasized the hopelessness of the case, the strong, almost masculine hands erupting from the sleeves of the habit like the inquisitive head of a prairie dog popping out of his hole.

Attempting to share the feelings of unreality which had engulfed me for so many months. I stemmed the tide of lament with a question. "You're quite sure that his mother won't be back?"

"I have written many letters—many letters and no replies. She lived in Hamburg. I was told the bombing there was very heavy. The War has disrupted postal communications, but the last three letters were returned. After her husband died, she left France because her parents urged her to move back home. Already in Germany, even before this, this," the speaker hesitated, groping for an image graphic enough to describe the occupation of France, "This desecration of our soil with German boots, there was a persecution of the Jewish people. Hilda feared her baby's blood would subject them to difficulty with the government."

The nun sighed, remembering a mother's anguish over abandoning an infant who represented the last tie with a husband, the only glimmer of light on the darkness of a Nazi horizon. Hastily dismissing the unpleasantness, she continued. "But he is handsome and healthy, and already very quick at his lessons."

I was aware that Sister Theresa was speaking so urgently because she was afraid. Afraid that this must-be-wealthy-because-she's-an-American woman would leave without solving the problem, solve it by removing another mouth to feed when funds were so scarce. The woolen material of my best dress chafed across my shoulders.

The directrice continued to sing the child's praises, while, unheeding, I turned to glance at the empty chair beside me. David should be sitting there, spruce and handsome in his blue uniform, smiling as he had when he waved good-bye to me at the train station. But because a burning plane had gone down into the cool waters of the English Channel, the chair remained vacant.

"May I see him?" I cut into the babble of assurances about the quality of the food and care given each child, my level tone concealing the painful squeeze in my chest which made it difficult to draw a breath.

The nun allowed an expression of immense relief to whisk across her scrubbed features and glanced at the clock. An important plateau had been reached; I could almost read her thoughts. It would have been much easier to refuse the child without having to watch him taste the possible rejection.

She rose. "Come, they will be at their recreation."

Sister Theresa whisked me out of the barren little room and into a dark corridor as though afraid her visitor would change her mind summarily and sail back to America. Dropping little personal tidbits behind her like the bread crumb trail left for Hansel and Gretel, the nun led the way. "He was only three months old when his mother left him with us. His birthday is in December. He will be six."

Half of My Heart

The gray and white robes whispered over the stone floor, worn smooth by the passage of many tiny feet. I could not shake the sensation of participating in a play, as though another woman inhabited my body, spoke confidently in response to questions. My only acting experience had been in the town pageant two years ago and in the trauma of confronting friends and neighbors across the stage, I had forgotten my speech. I needed David at my side to throw me the lifeline of my next cue; his letter had placed this burden upon me. Each phrase of that letter was burned into my memory; I could recite it word for word, close my eyes and see his scrawls across the tablet page.

> "Darling Jenny, the strangest and most wonderful thing happened today! Our jeep broke down in a town near Vichy and we had to wait hours for the parts from the base. I heard children laughing and looked over a stone wall and into an orphanage play yard. The orphanage is run by Catholic nuns and they invited us in. There was one baby lying in a basket on the grass, chuckling at a secret joke. I went over to share it with him and one of the sisters who spoke English told me that the baby's mother had left him and moved back to Germany. His father was a Jew who'd been killed in a car accident a few months after the baby was born. He had the most startling blue eyes, Jen, just like mine. I held him for a long time and he fell asleep. I know we promised my father that we'd have lots of grandsons to help run the farm, but it wouldn't hurt to get a head start on our family. If his mother doesn't come back, his life will be very hard because of his mixed heritage. I fell in love with him, Jen, he was so trusting and brave. When the parts for the jeep came, they had to pry his fingers away from my uniform lapel, but he didn't cry. I promised him I would be back after the war to get him and left collateral to reassure him. When we

wed, you promised to give me your heart. I left half of it in those clutching baby fingers. His name is Simon."

The remembrance of David's earnestness plus the fact that it was the last letter received before the somber telegram, which began, "The War Department regrets…" filled my eyes with tears and I blinked them away. Ever since I had first realized that David wasn't coming home with a duffel bag slung over his shoulder and a crooked smile on his dear, familiar features, an anger mixed with a throbbing loss filled my being.

David's parents had been wonderful, never once revealing the sorrow generated from allowing David's new bride, a constant reminder of his absence, to remain in their home. Determined to make a new beginning, I had continued in my teaching job at the school, tutoring pupils at night whenever possible, saving with the grim obsession of a miser.

An announcement over the potato soup one evening of my intention to sail to France and adopt Simon had startled Mother Holverson into dropping a platter. The thick china had splintered over the floor, while the words held inside for many months poured over the confines of the dam of reserve.

"No, Jenny! That's just foolishness! How can you take on that responsibility? You're still just a child yourself! How will you live? Do you expect to stay here? People will talk, say that it's David's child you've brought back. He's part German, isn't he? There will be hard feelings from the neighbors, everyone knows someone who was killed… Foolishness, foolishness! A child! Jennifer, you must reconsider. Think of our position…"

Think of my pain! Was that the anguished cry beneath the torrent of rambling words? A grandmother's dreams for David's family had already been destroyed; she could not bear the thought of loving and losing another child.

David's father had said nothing, his weather-seamed features remaining non-committal. When the news came of David's death, Father

Half of My Heart

Holverson's reaction had been to walk out to the field to finish plowing after comforting his two women.

David had inherited his father's gift of acceptance; compassion ran still and deep within Father Halverson. When I went up to my bedroom after helping to wash the supper dishes, there was a rusted soup can on the dressing table. It was filled with silver dollars and a few gold pieces, Jonathon Holverson's retirement money, formerly buried in the safeness of the back yard by the well house instead of entrusted to a bank, unearthed as a mute testimony of his support.

There was much to do and no time for tears. Three months later found me clad in one of the dresses I had stitched together after the day's chores were done, numbly trailing the authoritative figure of the directrice into the soft May sunshine, my quest almost at an end. The long days spent on the ship, the indifference of strangers and the sleepless nights were forgotten in the anticipation of meeting Simon.

There were over twenty children playing in the huge fenced-in area, rapid French shattering the pace, voices raised in shrieks of glee and anger as they fought over battered toys and hurtled themselves about in the joyous abandon of youth.

My strained nerves flinched at the uproar; although accustomed to the chatter of classroom, I realized that I had been mentally prepared for rows of sweet orphans singing rounds, with a spotlight on a baby lying in a basket on the grass. A golden haze should surround the children, with perhaps a sprinkling of violets to add color to the scene. But Simon was no longer a baby and this wasn't one of the musicals I had loved to attend on David's arm; there would be no bright and happy ending filled with song.

A child with a smudged face tore past in pursuit of another taunting sprite, dodging around my stiff, apprehensive figure with arrogant ease.

The directrice halted her brisk stride and surveyed the surging, healthy rabble with pride. I spotted Simon first, my gaze drawn to an aloof island surrounded by a turbulent sea.

He stood by the wall, his hands busy in the rhythmic action of tossing a ball against the stones and catching it. He held himself proudly, a short and sturdy five year old, bouncing a ball.

Christine Arness

The boy, my boy, turned with a defiant air as we approached. Simon had already discovered that life would be hard, that he would be scorned and called names, his parents reviled as German lovers—Jew lovers by the older children. His parentage was a dark stain on his record, blotting out any possibility of adoption. I could sense the hopeless despair which filled him.

Awaiting rebuke for not joining in with the others, Simon studied my hesitant figure standing behind the directrice with a defensive curiosity which I understood. So far, he had only been viewed by potential adoptive parents with pity or revulsion—not love.

"Simon, this is Jennifer Holverson. She's come all the way from America to see you!" The nun's voice carried the magic word over the roar which was instantly switched off as children spun to eye my foreign looking skirt and coat, the straight fall of wheat colored hair to my shoulders.

Murmurs of awe, "America!" were audible from the older children. Simon waited in stony silence, refusing to raise hopes that might be dashed, ignoring, I suddenly realized, the wisps of daydreams that had so often clothed him with two parents and a loving home.

I couldn't take my gaze from the dark features that must have been his father's legacy, the startlingly blue eyes which had captured David's attention.

Noting the sullen air of the rebel, I was suddenly flooded with the realization that this would not be easy. We shared many hidden scars, those of loneliness, helpless anger and fear of what the future might bring. He carried German blood in his veins, and I was jolted by a surge of white-hot fury at those who had murdered my David.

Loving Simon would mean abandoning the anger which still gripped my spirit at the shattering of a sparkling future, the betrayal of my own dreams. Mother Holverson had been right—I hadn't thought this mad project through. My only goal had been to see David once more in the person of Simon, fulfilling David's promise to an infant in order to selfishly find peace.

Sensing my withdrawal, Simon turned back to his solitary game. The thud of the ball had a desolate sound which echoed in my already aching heart. I remembered David's laughing words on paper that he had entrusted a portion of my heart promised him on our wedding day to Simon's keeping. Perhaps this division was responsible for my inability to heal those wounds of grief and despair or to look to the future with hope.

Suddenly, it was as though David's strong arm was around me once more, his tender support sweeping away my uncertainty. Raising Simon would be difficult. It would mean laying aside my sorrow and self-pity, placing Simon's welfare first, forgiving the legacy of hatred which he would bring to the peaceful farm. Buy my days were barren and meaningless without David. Part of my soul had been buried with David on foreign soil, the rest was clutched in the grimy fingers of the boy before me.

"I would like to adopt Simon. Please start the paperwork immediately." My voice sounded loud and confident, conveying the promise to the listening ears of the boy's tormentors that he was wanted, that wonders would be accomplished and he would go to America.

His body stiffened at the words; disbelief struggled with hope across his features. Revealing a desperate yearning for acceptance, Simon took a hesitant step nearer his rescuer and paused. The universe had shrunk around us, walling off the curious stares of the children and the shepherding nuns.

Intense blue eyes locked with the brown gaze of a woman from Kansas, a silent message passing between us as I extended my hand.

"I need you, Simon," I confided softly. "You see, you have half of my heart."

THE END

Short and Sweet

Ever since my father announced that he had enrolled in clown college, the words, "I have a surprise for you", ties my stomach into the knots first formed when he chaperoned my fourth grade Halloween party. I remember cringing while watching my parent demonstrate the proper technique of bobbing for apples. His hairy legs stuck out from under a sheet toga, a vegetable grater hung on a cord around his neck and he wore a name tag reading "Alex".

"What!" he bellowed, when one of my classmates timidly inquired who he was supposed to be. "You kids never heard of Alexander the Great?"

Thirty years later, I found myself doing deep breathing exercises to stave off an anxiety attack as I turned my car into Dad's driveway. My sister, Ellen, had declined to accompany me on the feeble grounds of keeping her two youngest children from scratching their chicken pox.

Smelling faintly of pizza, although it was barely 9:00 a.m., my father met me at the door and enveloped me in the traditional bear hug which had so disastrously rearranged my upswept hairdo the night of my senior prom.

"Glad you could come, Sweet Charlotte."

In supplying the information for my birth certificate, Dad had been struck by the way that combination of names fell on the ear—like Diamond and Jim as he later explained to my horrified mother. Instead of the innocuous Charlotte Ann, I am lumbered with the title of a Bette Davis movie.

Short and Sweet

With his arm draped around my shoulders, he steered me into the house. "Take a load off your legs, honey. I'll bring in the surprise."

My brain feverishly interpreted his words. The surprise at least was a solid object. I eliminated his having taken up hang gliding, opened a Greek restaurant or entered a lumberjack competition. Whatever it was, I wouldn't be surprised. Shocked out of my socks, perhaps ...

He bustled into the kitchen and the subsequent rustling noises conjured up images of a mouse trapped in a filing cabinet. My father was a retired carpenter, but insisted on popping out of society's confines of retirement with the unexpectedness of a jack-in-the-box.

"Close your eyes!" Dad's thinning hair had surrendered to advancing years, but his vocal projection remained undaunted.

I obeyed, thankful that long exposure had proven my heart capable of withstanding shocks of up to 6.8 on the Richter scale.

"Sweet Charlotte, meet Sugar."

Sugar? Wasn't that the name of the waitress he'd brought over for Thanksgiving dinner last year, the one who demonstrated her ability to chew gum and turkey at the same time? No, he couldn't have ...

My eyes snapped open and I recoiled, a disoriented Alice watching her toes recede into the distance in Wonderland. Patting the arm of my chair, I tried to reassure myself that the chair hadn't shrunk to doll house size beneath me.

I was nose to nose with the Tom Thumb of the equine world. I blinked. Chestnut coat, four legs, ears, mane, silky tail. A full grown horse that barely measured up to Dad's brass belt buckle.

My father chuckled. I think he has convinced himself over the years that I assume these grotesque expressions of disbelief solely for his amusement.

"Ain't she a beaut? Her fancy name is Bambi's Sugar and Spice."

I pointed a quivering finger. "Dad, that's a horse!"

"From the moment when as a mere babe in arms you called your Uncle Frank "Uncle Fink", I knew no one was ever gonna pull the wool over your eyes, Sweet Charlotte."

I forced a question through gritted teeth. "Where did you get this animal?"

"You oughta get out of the house more, girl! A miniature horse show was at the fairgrounds this weekend and Sugar's owner keeled over from a bad ticker. His daughter—reminded me of you, dear—showed up and wanted to get rid of the 'beast' immediately."

"A horse? In the house?"

"Now you sound like your mother, God rest her blessed soul. This little gal lets me sleep late, brings in the morning paper and, if she'll pardon the pun, don't nag. Can't say that 'bout most women."

Dad glanced around at the comfortably untidy living room, the newspapers strewn across the sofa, pipe tobacco spilled on the coffee table and the chess board set up for his weekly match with Doc Sims. "'Tain't noticed she's disrupted my housekeepin' much."

"Is she housetrained?"

"Back yard's fenced in." His eyes almost disappeared into laugh crinkles.

"I suppose you cut a pet door in the kitchen?"

Sarcasm bounced off Dad like pebbles flung against a rhino's hide. "She lifts the latch with her teeth and lets herself out. Sugar loves to do tricks. Bow, Sugar."

The thistledown delicate creature bobbed her head.

"Tell Sweet Charlotte your age."

The tapping of a hoof which appeared no bigger than a pencil eraser next to Dad's size fourteen work boots informed me that his new housemate was two years old.

My fond parent nudged me. "Hold out your hand."

Dating from an unfortunate experience at summer camp involving a mare with teeth the size of a bear trap, I have conceded the right-of-way to horses. Now my own flesh and blood expected me to offer my fingers within easy chomping range.

Realizing Eric would laugh himself into an aneurysm upon hearing that his wife had shown fear of this miniscule beastie, (and believe me, Dad would tell him all the details), I held out my hand and, through great effort, managed to keep it from quivering.

"Shake, Sugar," Dad commanded.

Sugar began a shimmying dance, wiggling her hips and shoulders in time to inaudible music. This time my stunned expression almost brought Dad to his knees in hysteria.

Short and Sweet

"It's a joke, see, sweetie? You think she's gonna hold her hoof up like a dog does his paw, but instead Sugar shakes her whole body. Isn't it a hoot?"

"A hoot and a half," I murmured in feeble agreement.

He insisted on taking me on a tour of the filly's sleeping quarters. Mom would have given up the ghost years earlier if she'd foreseen the conversion of her beloved sewing room into a stall complete with a manger. Sugar followed Dad like his shadow, her hooves clicking on the faded linoleum and ears pricked forward within scratching distance of his gnarled fingers.

Once again, I was the Tin Man, condemned to stand in the forest of confusion planted by my father, with my jaw rusted open in perpetual surprise. Upon seeing that Mom's Haviland china soup tureen had been pressed into service as a water bowl, I mumbled some excuse about a dentist appointment and fled.

As Eric brushed his teeth that evening, I shouted my woes over the sound of running water.

He came out of the bathroom toweling his face dry. "I don't see the problem, Char. The horse is smaller than a Great Dane. Be thankful he didn't fill the backyard with sand and raise ostriches."

"A horse is snoring next to Mom's sewing machine and you're making jokes?"

My understanding hubby slipped under the blankets. "I don't know why you're so upset. I had the guts to marry you, even after your father released a live 'dove of peace' during the ceremony. Remember how that bird made a direct hit on the pastor's shiny black hair?" He started to laugh.

Remember? My wedding album contained an action shot of the incident, the last picture ever taken with that particular lens. The photographer had chortled so hard that he'd dropped his camera ...

After her introduction to Dad's new live-in companion, my sister reported that Sugar was adjusting nicely to suburban life. "She's adorable, Char. Just be thankful he didn't invite a sumo wrestler to share the house."

"But a horse, Ellen? Why can't we have a normal parent—I've always wanted a father who checked his investments in the Wall Street

Journal each morning and spent his afternoons on the golf course."

"I grew up thinking other fathers were dull. You can't confine Dad inside the rigid lines of respectability."

"Respectability? I'll settle for a little bit less eccentricity …"

My sister ignored my mutterings. "Dad's built a cart and gets his exercise giving the neighborhood children rides. Pudgy little Beth Armstrong's mother is thrilled—until Beth loses ten pounds she's been limited to only grooming Sugar, and last night, Beth refused cherry pie at supper. She's a motivated little girl"

"Great. Beth Armstrong can't eat and I can't sleep."

Ellen chuckled. "To me, having Dad around is like living on a fault line. You never know when the big quake is going to hit …

I soon discovered that I couldn't show my face in public, either. Dad, resplendent in baggy pants, a rubber nose and grease paint, was a regular entertainer at a local children's hospital. By some bizarre slicing of red tape, he managed to receive permission to make a joint appearance with Sugar.

The duo's picture appeared on the front page of the Variety section of the Minneapolis Star Tribune Sunday paper, with Sugar tapping out the days until his birthday for a little boy with a big cast and equally huge eyes. The caption read, "Putting Their Best Foot Forward to Make Others Laugh."

I cringed, guiltily grateful that the grease paint and rubber nose concealed Dad's features. My beaming father presented me with a framed copy of the photograph which I hung in the dining room, a constant reminder of my wretchedness in wanting to subdue his free spirit.

Of course, rain was bound to fall on this happy parade. Somehow it always did—Dad had a knack of bringing the thunder. The first shower came from Dad's neighbor, Mrs. Johansen, a sweet-faced widow in her late sixties. My private fantasy has been to see her and my father rocking in synchronized rhythm on his front porch—Mrs. Johnsen knitting while Dad held the yarn and extra needles.

If Mrs. Johansen cherished any romantic dreams, however, she pursued them on the level of a third grade boy putting a frog in the desk of his beloved. When Dad hired a Jamaican band to celebrate his

Short and Sweet

birthday, Mrs. Johnsen called the police and complained about the heathen orgy next door. She baked Dad's favorite meal, deep dish beef and onion pie, and left the pie cooling on her window sill where the tempting aroma drifted into a bachelor's home and spoiled the taste of a solitary hamburger.

"She leaves the sweet pickles out, too," Dad grumbled. "I sneaked a piece once and told her the crows must have done it. She yelled so loud she blistered the paint on my house. That old battle-axe could sour cotton candy."

My curiosity regarding her reaction to the stable next door was answered by an early morning call from Dad. His voice shook and for a moment I thought something had happened to Ellen.

"Dad? What's wrong? Please, tell me what's going on!"

Eric was on his way out the door, but paused in response to my frantic arm motions. When at last I hung up and cradled my head in my hands, my husband headed for the medicine cabinet and the antacid tablets.

He swallowed two. "Give it to me straight, Char. I can take it."

"Mrs. Johansen complained to City Hall about Sugar and Dad received notice that he must get rid of her within thirty days. I promised him you'd look into it."

My wonderful attorney husband cancelled two appointments and spent the morning at City Hall looking for loopholes before calling me with his findings. Black clouds of gloom trailed my car like exhaust fumes as I drove to a nursing home where Dad and Sugar were performing, wondering how I could break the news.

Standing in back of an obstacle course of wheelchairs and canes, I waved at Dad, who was sporting fire engine red suspenders dating from his honeymoon, baggy pants and a battered derby. Sugar, looking like she'd stepped down from a kiddie carousel, stood at his side.

"This fantastic filly will now astound you with her mathematical abilities. Do I have a volunteer?"

A man whose wrinkles indicated he could have been a boyhood chum of Herbert Hoover raised a palsied hand.

"This young man wishes to have Sugar, the Wonder Horse, guess his age," Dad barked in his best W. C. Fields tones. There was a faint chuckle here and there, a ripple moving through those assembled like a breeze through reeds by the water's edge.

"Sugar, take a good look at this man."

Sugar studied the man with an intelligent gaze.

"Wonder Horse, count his age."

Sugar blew through her nostrils in a snort of obvious disbelief. Her little knees quivered, buckled and suddenly she was lying on her back with four tiny hooves waving in the air.

"Ah, yesss. The prospect of counting all those years has caused the Wonder Horse to pass out." Dad's face mirrored exaggerated disgust.

The ripple became a wave of mirth, frail shoulders shaking, wrinkled hands held to mouths, white heads bobbing.

The pat phrases I had been assembling in my mind, "A horse isn't a practical pet, is it?" and "You'll have to face facts," crumbled along with my composure, and I hurried outside to shed a few tears over the azalea bushes.

Dad and Sugar appeared half an hour later. "I had to pry her out with a crow bar," he apologized.

I gave him Eric's findings and he stood silent. Unable to bear the pain in his eyes, I looked at the little mare who had dropped her head to snatch a mouthful of grass and found myself sniffing.

Dad put his arm around me, and I drew comfort from the strength of his bear hug. "'Tain't fair," he muttered, kicking at a crack in the sidewalk. "She's no bigger than Dick Thompson's Great Dane and don't yap like Miz Percy's poodle."

"Eric says the city ordinances prohibit livestock in a residential area. Horses, no matter how small, are currently classified as livestock."

Jealous, Sugar nuzzled Dad's hand for attention. He fingered a velvety ear. "There's more than one way to fatten a hog. I read in the paper last week that the mayor's kids have themselves a pet monkey."

I hated to dash his hopes. "A monkey is classified as an exotic animal—permitted if the owner obtains the consent of his neighbors and the City Council. But Sugar is a horse—not a zebra."

Dad snapped his suspenders against his chest. "Keep your chin up, Sweet Charlotte. I'll think of somethin'. The old brain box ain't short-circuited yet." He gave me a final hug before trudging towards his van

Short and Sweet

with its built-in stall, Sugar trotting on his heels like a well-trained puppy.

Although I had longed for a more sedate parent, I couldn't sleep that night, picturing a shrunken version of Dad slumped on the front porch and rocking the rest of his life away. I tried to punch my pillow and got Eric's shoulder instead.

"I've been thinking, darling—"

"Try not to think so violently," my husband mumbled.

"If Dad loses Sugar, it will break his spirit."

"Relax, Char. You're talking about a man whose own father single-handedly captured ten German soldiers and, by the time reinforcements arrived, had them singing "The Star Spangled Banner" in four-part harmony. You come from tough stock. This is a minor setback."

"Maybe he could board Sugar at a stable—"

"If push comes to shove, Char, we'll explore that possibility, but tonight I need my sleep."

So did I. Eric called me from the office the next morning. "Brace yourself, honey. Your dad asked me to get him on the agenda for tonight's City Council meeting. He's got a 'surprise' for them."

We arrived at City Hall just before 7:00 p.m., after a stop at the drug store to pick up another package of antacid tablets for Eric's stomach. Ellen's youngest now had the chicken pox, but she had made a solemn vow to light a candle in the window and keep vigil until we returned.

We found Dad seated in the front row, dressed in the blue suit purchased for my wedding more years ago than I cared to remember. He hugged me and audibly cracked Eric's ribs before allowing us to take our places on the chairs he'd been saving.

"What's your strategy?" I hissed across Eric's shirtfront as my husband checked to make sure his antacid tablets hadn't been crushed.

Dad shrugged. "I'll just appeal to their better natures." He watched the members file in and take their places at the council table, nary a smile or a laugh wrinkle among the lot of them.

He added soberly, "Course, I might need a steam shovel to dig through them layers of orneriness—that one woman looks like someone mixed quick drying cement in with her face powder."

The agenda was crowded and we had a long wait. At intervals I glanced over at my father in his ill-fitting blue suit, the hands gnarled from years of labor resting in his lap. I reflected on how Dad's education had never progressed past his junior year in high school because his own father's death had made him the family breadwinner. Dad was a simple man pitted against the brick wall of bureaucracy. A simple man ... After a few more memories, I began to pity the council members.

When they called Dad's name, he rose and grabbed the microphone like a veteran entertainer. Stating his name, he handed over a stack of permission slips signed by every resident on his block.

"How did he get Mrs. Johansen's signature?" I whispered.

Eric winced inside his suit and fumbled for another tablet. "Don't ask, Char."

"Comparin' Sugar with regular horses is like saying there ain't no difference whether you're squeezing basketball players or babies into a phone booth." My father's voice boomed over the murmur of the audience, silencing those who had prepared to discuss other issues during his presentation.

But the council members were not as polite. Some doodled on scratch pads while others seemed on the verge of nodding off. As Dad finished his speech with an impassioned plea, a stout man leaned over to whisper a comment to the city attorney, who chuckled.

My fingernails dug into my palms, and I put the brakes on my rising blood pressure by mentally sketching campaign posters and composing slogans to boot the inconsiderate louts out of office.

The mayor lifted the permit application gingerly, as if the paper had been contaminated by a plague victim. "I'm sorry, Mr. Lloyd. Permission can only be granted for an exotic animal. The animal in question is a horse. This matter should never have been placed on the agenda."

Bang! The gavel signaled dismissal of the man tugging at the too tight collar of an out-of-date suit. Tears sprang into my eyes, and I leaped to my feet to protest. Eric yanked me back down, apparently visualizing his legal career and community standing shot down in flames.

"Excuse me, Your Honor." Dad looked as if he'd bitten into a lemon. I recognized that pucker—he was unsuccessfully trying to

Short and Sweet

discipline a grin. "If I can prove that Sugar is an exotic animal, will you grant my permit?"

The city attorney tipped his chair back on two legs. "Mr. Lloyd, if you can prove that horse is an exotic animal, nothing stands in the way of your permit," he drawled.

Dad said, "God bless America" for no apparent reason, saluted our nation's flag hanging behind the council table and disappeared through the double doors at the rear of the room. Eric crossed himself, despite his ancestors having embraced Methodism, while I gripped the handle of my handbag.

The doors reopened.

Eric and I were on our feet with the rest of the audience, craning our necks at the spectacle of a miniature horse with a grass skirt draped across her middle and a lei of purple flowers encircling her dainty neck.

Dad led Sugar up to the long table. Sugar gazed at the council members; the council members stared back, their expressions as deadpan as gunfighters meeting on a dusty western street.

Dad released his grip on the bridle. "Shake, Sugar."

Sugar broke into her bump and grind routine, shoulders and hips swaying to the beat of inaudible island drums, the grass skirt fluttering and lei bobbing.

My father's eyes gleamed in triumph, a modern day John Paul Jones shaking his fist in the teeth of enemy fire. "Well, folks? Name me an item that's more exotic than a hula dancer!"

For a heartbeat, the silence was so profound you could have heard a spider cough.

Then the city attorney choked and his chair crashed backwards to the floor, taking him with it. The mayor's lips twitched. One of the younger council members dissolved into giggles, putting her head down on crossed arms in a spasm of helpless laughter.

Dad's hearty bass led an avalanche of sound as men slapped each other on the back, chortling and pointing, while women tee-heed behind matronly hands. I sagged against my husband, who mopped his brow and grinned. The city attorney's careless promise had given Eric better grounds for a suit than a Mr. Coffee if the permit was refused.

But the wall of bureaucracy recognized the overwhelming force of the wrecking ball. His Honor waved the gavel in a feeble arc, a wooden flag of surrender, and gasped between chuckles. "Permission granted, Mr. Lloyd."

The reporter covering the proceedings rushed up to take a picture of the "exotic" animal. The mayor held Sugar's bridle, heroically refraining from wincing when a sharp hoof mashed his toes, while my father beamed in the background.

Swallowing the lump in my throat, I pushed my way through the milling throng and threw my arms around my father. "I'm proud of you, Dad."

"Watch that bear hug, Sweet Charlotte! You could hurt a man." He felt his ribs with tender concern.

Dad was Dad. He'd always been and would be until the day he no longer enlivened my humdrum existence.

The lump was back in my throat and I spoke with difficulty. "Ellen wants us all to come over for coffee and cake, Dad. We'll have a victory party."

He looked sheepish. "Gotta take a rain check, honey. Ms. Johansen's fixin' me a deep dish beef and onion pie with sweet pickles. A man needs a little variety in his life."

THE END

About the Author

Lori Ness wrote her first novel when she ran out of books that she liked to read. Rosemary for Remembrance, published by Harper Paperbacks under the pseudonym Christine Arness, was nominated for a Romantic Times Award for Best Contemporary Romantic Novel. Her second book, Wedding Chimes, Assorted Crimes, was a hardcover published by Five Star. Lori has also published numerous articles, short stories, newspaper articles and essays.

www.christinearness.com

Also available by the author

A Cozy Country Christmas
Fairy Christmas, Darling
"In for a Penny" and "Breath of God" in Romance and Mystery Under the Northern Lights, An Anthology

Made in the USA
San Bernardino, CA
17 February 2015